THE
Stepmom
SHAKE-
Up

ALSO BY NIKI LENZ

Bernice Buttman, Model Citizen

THE
Stepmom
SHAKE-
Up

Niki Lenz

Random House New York

Grateful acknowledgment is made to The Ronald Reagan Presidential Foundation and Institute for permission to reprint excerpt from Ronald Reagan letter to Nancy Reagan. Used by permission of The Ronald Reagan Presidential Foundation and Institute. All rights reserved.

Visit us on the Web! rhcbooks.com

Educators and librarians, for a variety of teaching tools, visit us at RHTeachersLibrarians.com

Library of Congress Cataloging-in-Publication Data
Name: Lenz, Niki, author.
Title: The stepmom shake-up / Niki Lenz.
Description: First edition. | New York : Random House, [2020] | Summary: When her widowed father threatens the integrity of Team Gravy by starting to date again, twelve-year-old Grace decides to sabotage all his romantic endeavors.
Identifiers: LCCN 2019019762 (print) | LCCN 2019022400 (ebook) |
ISBN 978-1-9848-9254-6 (trade) | ISBN 978-1-9848-9256-0 (library binding) |
ISBN 978-1-9848-9255-3 (ebook)
Subjects: CYAC: Fathers and daughters—Fiction. | Family life—Fiction. |
Dating (Social customs)—Fiction. | Clergy—Fiction.
Classification: LCC PZ7.1.L45 St 2020 (print) | LCC PZ7.1.L45 (ebook) | DDC [Fic]—dc23

Printed in the United States of America
10 9 8 7 6 5 4 3 2 1
First Edition

Random House Children's Books supports the First Amendment and celebrates the right to read.

To Caleb, who tells the best Dad Jokes,
to Loralie and her wild outfits,
and to Roman, who really put bleach in the washing
machine when he was a toddler.
I love being on a team with you.

CONTENTS

THE Stepmom SHAKE-Up

1

Space for Possibilities

The Christmas tree teetered on the edge of disaster as Dad and I heaved it up the tight attic staircase.

"You got it?" Dad's muffled voice came from behind the box he was shoving through the door.

"Um, sort of?" I said, trying to get a good grip on the box.

"Come on, Grace, use those muscles!" Dad said, and then he gave the box a last big push and he and the Christmas tree tumbled onto the rough wooden floor.

"Whew," he said, wiping sweat and dust from his face. "Hey, Grace, why did the muscle miss class?"

I itched my nose. "I feel a dad joke coming on. . . ."

"Because it wasn't a tendon." Dad smiled, his mouth and eyes wide, waiting for me to burst into laughter.

Instead I groaned. "Remind me again why we don't just leave that thing set up all the time?"

Dad shrugged. Our beagle, Potus, had squeezed past me and was happily sniffing around a mountain of cardboard boxes. "It's bigger up here than I remembered . . . ," I said.

Dad snorted and shoved the Christmas tree box toward the far wall. The attic has vaulted ceilings and two dirty windows that face the front of the house. The piles of junk were balanced on plywood to keep them from falling through the unfinished floor. I brushed a spiderweb out of my hair without flinching. "I like it."

Dad glanced at me with a puzzled look. "What exactly do you like?"

"This space! It's big up here. Way bigger than my room. It could fit a bunch more bookshelves, and maybe a couch. Plus, I could set up my sewing machine. . . ."

The sewing machine was a gift my grandma sent me last Christmas. My plan was to make historically accurate costumes so I could talk my dad into doing some cosplay. Technically, cosplay is when you dress up like characters from a movie, book, or video game, but I thought historical figures should count too. This attic space would give me room to really spread out, unlike my bedroom, which was basically a closet with a bed in it.

Dad scratched his head. "You want to clean this up?"

I grinned and bounced on my heels. "Fun project, huh? You've been saying we need a new one." Dad and I are always doing "projects." We'd just completed a deluxe dog condo for Potus and presented it to him with a big bow on it for Christmas. Potus was very impressed with our craftsmanship. He gave it two paws up.

Dad blew a raspberry, taking in the city of boxes, the cobwebs, and the unfinished—okay, fine, probably unsafe—status of the attic. "A *project* is right."

"Come on, can't you see it? We'll move this stuff to the basement. Add some walls and floors."

"And update the electrical, and add insulation, new light fixtures . . ." Dad ticked things off on his fingers, but I could see the wheels turning in his head. Once he caught the vision for things I wanted to create, I could usually drag him on board.

"Hmm," he said, which was as good as a yes. He reached into the nearest box and pulled out a dusty leather-bound book. "Some of this stuff has been up here for a very long time."

The house we live in once belonged to my grandparents. They gave it to my parents as a wedding present. It's over a hundred years old, full of creaks and quirks and cramped bedrooms that can't support the many hobbies of a sixth-grade girl.

"What about this: We finish this area and make it my room, and then you can have my old room for an office. You've always wanted an office. Think of all the space you would have to practice your sermons!"

Dad is the pastor of the First Baptist Church in town. He spends a lot of time poring over books on our dining room table and pacing in front of our living room couch inventing illustrations, those funny and often embarrassing little stories that are part of a sermon.

He flipped through the book in his hand, deep concentration screwing up his face. "I think this diary belonged to your four-times-great-grandmother. It says Juliet Martin here."

I leaned over and took a peek at the scrawled handwriting. "Cool!" The pages were all yellowy and water stained, and the date on the first entry was March 7, 1904. As I lifted the journal out of Dad's hands, a photograph freed itself from the pages and drifted to the floor. Potus sniffed at the picture and I bent to pick it up.

Dad's eyes widened. "That's a picture of Juliet!" Dad and I are both huge history buffs, and he has done a lot of research into our family tree. The girl in the picture didn't look much older than me. She wore a high-collar lace dress and held a parasol. Her lips curled into a mischievous smile. I flipped the picture over. She had scrawled on the back that it was taken on her sixteenth birthday at the St. Louis World's Fair. Great-Grandma had a wicked glint in her eye that made me wonder if she'd gotten into any trouble during her visit to the fair.

"What a find!" Dad said, shaking his head at the picture.

"There could be more cool stuff up here that we don't even know about. If we make this our latest and greatest project, we can go through everything, decide what to keep and what to get rid of. Plus, you'll get your new office. . . ."

I grinned at Dad, eyebrows raised in my most puppy-dog expression. Potus tilted his head adorably, although I doubted he even knew what we were begging for.

"Fine," Dad said, unable to resist our charm. "Grab a box and take it down with you. We've got a lot of junk to sift through."

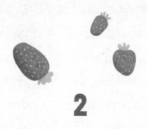

2

Sunday Funday

"Dad, your Pop-Tart is smoking," I yelled, pouring myself a nice, nonflaming bowl of Cocoa Puffs.

"What! No!" Dad barreled down the stairs, tie hanging loosely around his neck. "I set it at five!"

"Five minutes is too long for a Pop-Tart."

"Not minutes. Degrees of toastiness. Like on a scale of one to ten. So a five would be perfectly medium-ly toasted."

"We've had this discussion before," I said, my mouth full of cereal.

Dad gripped the toaster pastry by two fingers and flung it into the sink, then ran his burnt fingers under the cool water. "So cereal, then. Good choice."

I pushed the box across the table, and he dumped some in a bowl.

"And they say we need to learn how to cook." He grinned at me over the milk.

"Who says that?"

"They."

"Who are they?"

"People who say things."

I knew he was kidding, but it still bugged me a little. Ever since my mom died three years ago, people always try to tell Dad and me what we need to do.

"Got your sermon ready to go?"

Dad nodded. "I'm speaking on Psalm Thirty-Seven. The four *F*s of Christianity."

I raised my eyebrows. "And they are?"

He ticked off the points on his fingers. "*Fear not, fret not, faint not*, and . . . *fart not?*"

I choked, a Cocoa Puff going down the wrong pipe. "What!"

He squinted at something scribbled on his hand. "Oh, oops. I think that last one was *forget not*."

"Well, *forget not* the last *F*. And don't say *fart* in church." I smiled sweetly at him and shoveled a spoonful of cereal into my mouth.

"Don't worry, I'll make it clear as mud." Dad started to straighten his tie.

"Wait. Stop." I stared hard at the hideous tie hanging around his neck.

Dad glanced down at the red-and-green monstrosity. "You got me this for Christmas!"

"Dad, it's January. And it was kind of a joke."

"Oh, I see. Now that Christmas is over, we're supposed to forget all about the little baby Jesus's birthday?"

"Kinda." I nodded.

Dad sighed but pulled the tie off his neck. "What about your outfit?" His eyes narrowed at me.

I inspected my polka-dot leggings, my button-down shirt with the sequined birds, and my striped knee socks. "What's wrong with my outfit?"

"Never mind," he mumbled, and headed upstairs to get a less seasonal tie.

There was a knock at the kitchen door. Potus barked his fool head off until I shushed him. I flung the door open and threw my arms around my best friend, Bea.

"Hey, Team Gravy!" Bea said.

Team Gravy is this thing my dad made up by squishing our names together. *Grace* plus my dad's name, *Davy*. It's silly, but it sort of stuck.

Bea shuffled into the warm, messy kitchen. "I thought I'd catch a ride with you guys, since I gotta be at church early this morning." Her guitar case bumped against her leg, and her arms were full of sheet music.

Today she'd be performing a classical rendition of the Josh Groban hit "You Raise Me Up." Although completely against her rock-and-roll sentiment, it was the only song the deacons allowed from her list of suggestions. Luckily, no one was singing, so we wouldn't be subjected to the sappy words.

"Hey, come look at this!" I said, grabbing Bea's hand and dragging her to the pull-down attic stairs. She was all worried about spiders, but I managed to get her up there. "Can't you just see it?" I said as I walked her through the plans for the space. My eyes drifted from rafters to floor, and I pointed out where I'd put my bed, my bookshelves, my desk, and my sewing table.

"And where will you put your presidential bobbleheads?" Bea smirked. Side effect of being history-obsessed: I have collected thirty-nine presidential bobblehead dolls.

I tapped my chin. "We might have to fashion some sort of shelving unit just for that purpose."

Bea's eyebrows knit together. "Is it safe up here? I mean, are there smoke detectors and carbon monoxide detectors and a rope ladder in case you have to escape out the window?"

I laughed. Bea worries just like a grown-up sometimes. "Yeah, I promise, it will pass a safety inspection when we're done. Don't put your feet anywhere except on these cross boards for now. You'll go right through the ceiling."

She smiled. "Well, if anyone can turn this dusty mess into the world's coolest bedroom, it's you and your dad."

I grinned. "Thanks."

Bea looked at her watch. "We'd better get going. I wanna have time to warm up."

We loaded into Dad's black pickup, with Bea's guitar stowed in the back and her sheet music tucked between us. Our house is only three blocks from First Baptist, so some mornings we walk. But today it was pitch dark, plus it was drizzling and super cold, so we were grateful for the canned heat of the truck.

Silence tucked around us like a blanket as we passed the misty graveyard where my mom is buried. I didn't want to think about her in the ground when it was so cold outside. I had to keep reminding myself she wasn't really there at all. Her soul was having a good old time in heaven with Jesus.

Sometimes I'm super jealous of Jesus.

I don't cry much anymore. Not every single day, like I used to. Me and Dad have managed to find our own rhythm in the last three years. We feed ourselves (badly), we work (his sermons, my school stuff), and we entertain ourselves (by trying to see who can memorize the most random presidential facts). We've been doing okay, just so long as neither of us shook things up.

I watched the ice-slicked headstones fade in the fog as we turned the last corner and the church came into view.

First Baptist of Springdale is a large redbrick building off the main square in our smallish town. I say smallish, because we have a Walmart, and a couple of four-way stops, and a pretty big college that adds a few thousand people to our population during the school year. But there's only one high school, so me and my classmates will be together for the long haul. Too bad for Sammy, the kid who ate glue in kindergarten, because people don't forget stuff like that. Or stuff like you used to have a mom, but now you don't.

Dad parked the truck and helped Bea lift her case while I fumbled with the keys to get the main doors open. It's a small town but a big church, so we lock the doors when there isn't anything going on.

It was quiet and peaceful inside the empty building. Bea headed to the sanctuary to practice. I went to work flipping on lights while Dad cranked up the heat.

I know some kids don't like going to church. They'd rather have a second Saturday, playing sports or hanging out with friends. But I can't imagine my life without Sundays at church. This building, and the people who visit it on foggy, cold mornings, take up a huge part of my heart. I belong here, just as much as the Bibles and hymnals.

My feet paused in the hallway when I heard voices. Maybe a staff member had slipped in after us. Something about the hushed tone made me want to eavesdrop.

"Maybe you should just tell him. . . ."

"Tell Pastor Davy?"

"Yes."

"He should know."

A chill went up my spine. The voices were talking about my dad, and they seemed worried. And worried grown-up voices make my palms slick with sweat.

"Fine. Let's meet after service."

Footsteps clomped down the hall and disappeared up a stairway. I stayed frozen to the spot, wondering what in the world the pastor needed to know.

3

Whispers

When you're the preacher's kid, you're always the last person on the planet to get to leave the church after a service. My dad has to shake hands with every single member. He even takes a minute to pray with some people. I usually hang out in the back of the sanctuary, in the very last pew, bouncing my knees and wiggling my toes inside my too-tight shoes until he's finally done.

"Hey, Grace," a warm, familiar voice said over my shoulder.

I looked up from the notebook I was doodling in and smiled at Miss O'Connor, my history teacher.

"I like your picture. Is that James Madison?" she asked. Only Miss O'Connor would be able to pick our fourth president out of a lineup.

"Yeah. I've been working on drawings of the six presidents named James."

Miss O'Connor screwed up her face and squinted at the ceiling. "Madison, Monroe, Polk, Buchanan, Garfield, and Carter."

"That's correct. A-plus for you." I laughed as she plopped down next to me in the pew. Unlike most people who attend the First Baptist Church, Miss O'Connor doesn't do much to dress up for the Lord's Day. Her dark curls were crammed into a messy bun, and she wore jeans and a sparkly purple sweater.

"Your dad still telling the patrons to scram?"

"Ha ha."

"I liked his sermon today. It reminded me of that episode of *Jungle Survivor* when Donald gave his last ration of rice to Gabe, even though they weren't on the same team."

Everything reminded Miss O'Connor of an episode of *Jungle Survivor*. She obsessed about the show and had sent in audition videos approximately a million times. I know because I'd spent many a Sunday afternoon helping with the camerawork.

"He watched that episode when he practiced for today, so you may be onto something."

Miss O'Connor patted my knee and stood up again. "I'm off to wipe the boogers off the children's Bibles. See you in class tomorrow."

I smiled and nodded until I remembered Miss O'Connor had assigned an essay on the Pilgrims that I still hadn't started. Sunday nights are a sad ending to the weekend. They're all homework, and go to bed early, and blah, blah, blah.

My dad came in through the heavy double doors and said hi to Miss O'Connor as they passed each other. "There's the other half of Team Gravy!" He breezed past me to retrieve his notes from the pulpit. "One of the committees wanted to call a short meeting this afternoon." He tapped his papers into an orderly pile before placing them inside his leather binder.

The voices in the hallway.

My heart did a weird double bump in my chest.

"Which committee?" I asked, trying to make my voice sound normal.

He squinted up at the ceiling for a second before he said, "Uh, Building and Grounds, I think. Maybe they've found someone to fix the second-floor bathroom. . . ."

The Building and Grounds Committee mostly tries to keep up with the maintenance of our super-old church building. They're always attempting to get Dad to sign off on projects that the church doesn't really have the money for, like new carpet in the sanctuary and stuff like that. Could that be what the two voices in the hallway had been worried about?

Dad whistled as he bustled around the sanctuary. He'd settled on wearing his favorite blue tie, the one I'd given him last Father's Day, and a charcoal-gray suit. He'd changed his shiny black shoes already, switched out for his blue sneakers.

"So this meeting, did they tell you what it was about?" My stomach roared, demanding a trip to the pizza place for the all-you-can-eat lunch buffet.

Dad shook his head. "Would you mind straightening up in here while you wait?" He hopped down the three red-carpeted steps to the first pew just as the double doors opened and the Building and Grounds Committee marched in on cue.

There were only two of them. Miss Marge was a white-haired granny with round glasses, exactly like Mrs. Claus. The other lady, Miss Donna, was tall and wore her dark hair in a low bun. She reminded me of Popeye's girlfriend, Olive Oyl. Their shoes clumped down the center aisle past me, and I busied myself tucking hymnals back into place and picking up trash from the floor.

"Pastor Davy, thank you for coming to this meeting," Miss Marge said. I couldn't help but think we'd hardly had a choice about coming to the meeting.

Miss Donna piped up. "Great sermon today, Davy."

Usually, I think of these two like my own grandmothers. They're always patting my head and squeezing my cheeks, but they mean well. Like everyone else at the First Baptist

Church, I've known them my whole life. But the worry in their hushed voices earlier still sent a shiver of nervousness up my spine. Whatever they wanted to talk to Dad about had not sounded good.

"Please, sit." Dad gestured to the pews. It was an awkward seating arrangement, as Dad had to be twisted around to see them. I kept picking up hymnals and hoped they'd ignore me and get to the point.

"Pastor Davy, we just wanted to tell you that the church did manage to raise the funds to repaint the preschool classrooms. We should have that done by the end of the week."

I let out a breath. That wasn't so bad. New paint was good, right? So why all the whispering?

"Great. Thanks so much, ladies, for organizing all that," Dad said, but his face looked quizzical.

"There's been some talk around here, Davy—" Miss Marge started.

"Everyone just wants what's best for you, of course," Miss Donna interrupted.

"It's just that . . . well, the Bible says, *It is not good for man to be alone.*" Miss Marge's voice bounced around the vaulted ceiling of the sanctuary.

My dad laughed. "What do you mean, alone? I've got Grace. I'm never alone!"

"What we mean is," Miss Marge said kindly, "maybe

it's time you meet a nice young lady. And take her to the movies! Or a spaghetti dinner. My Carl always took me out for spaghetti."

"And when you find the one," Miss Donna added in a low voice, like she was letting Dad in on a big secret, "you gotta put a ring on it."

I dropped the hymnal I had gripped in my hands. When everyone swiveled to look at me, I bent to pick it up from the floor and stayed hidden between the pews.

Put a ring on it? Were they suggesting that my dad get *married?* They couldn't be serious! Why would my dad want to do that? We were perfectly happy just the way we were. I peeked over the edge of the pew to watch Dad tell them off.

"That's not as easy as it sounds," Dad said, a crooked smile on his face. Not exactly the outraged argument I'd expected, but at least he wasn't agreeing. His eyes searched the back pews until they landed on me, and all the color drained from his face.

Dad cleared his throat. "Is that all of the official Building and Grounds Committee business? The paint, I mean."

The ladies looked sheepish. Miss Donna especially. She had bright pink dots high on her cheekbones. But she held her head high. "I'm going to be real honest, Pastor. That last part, about you finding a lady . . . that wasn't committee business at all. Just two old broads who like to meddle in other people's private lives."

Miss Marge elbowed Miss Donna in the ribs, but then turned her angelic face to my dad. "You shouldn't hide away from the world, Pastor. You deserve love. You and Grace both. Maybe it's time to give it a chance?"

I stuffed the hymnal into the holder and sidestepped out of the pew, catching my dad's eye as I stomped through the double doors of the sanctuary. He followed me to his truck and got in the driver's side.

"You can't even be thinking about this!" I said, slamming the passenger door shut and crossing my arms over my chest. "There's nobody in this town good enough to be your girlfriend! You don't even *want* a girlfriend!"

Dad gripped the steering wheel, and a look passed over his face that I didn't understand. "If you want to be an expert on what I want, you'll just have to get in line."

I think my mouth actually flew open, but no words came out.

Of course I knew what my dad wanted.

I knew him better than anyone.

He didn't want a girlfriend, and he'd already had a wife.

And we don't let people boss us around.

His voice softened then, his eyes crinkling around the edges. "Miss Donna and Miss Marge seem to think it's time for me to start considering . . . I don't know, getting out there. Trying again. Meeting new people."

I was stunned. I was a cow that had wandered too close to the electric fence. I was a deer in the headlights. I was a mouse snapped in a spring-loaded trap, gripping my cheese.

Dad laughed at the shocked look on my face. "I thought Miss Donna made some pretty compelling points."

I felt the heat creep up my neck. "Like what?"

Dad shrugged. "I don't know."

"Yes you do."

He let out a breath. "Having someone to take out for a nice spaghetti dinner! Being a pastor and a single dad, I get lonely sometimes. To tell you the truth, I've been thinking about this for a while now."

My dad was not lonely. "You can't be lonely! You have me. We're always together."

He turned toward me and squeezed my shoulder. "You are the very best thing in my whole life. And I love you with every single fiber of my being. But it is not the same as being . . . in love."

I swallowed hard and turned my face to the window.

This couldn't be the truth.

My dad was happy.

We were happy.

Dad pulled the truck into the parking lot of Ziggy's Italian Pizzeria, and we sat in the warm cab.

"So, you're going to go on dates and, like, get married?"

"Well, yes to dates. Let's not get too far ahead of ourselves about marriage."

The smell of delicious pizza hung heavy in the air. There was already a long line for the lunch buffet, but my body and brain seemed frozen.

"Listen, you don't need to worry about this, Grace. The church ladies have just given me a little kick in the pants to get out there and date. So . . . can I get out there and date?"

The thought of him going on dates, trying to find someone as awesome as Mom . . . it made my stomach churn. But my dad's blue eyes looked so dang hopeful, I couldn't help but nod.

He rubbed his belly. "I'm starving. Let's get our money's worth out of this buffet."

I cracked a weak smile.

Dad pulled the keys out of the ignition. "Hey, how do you fix a broken pizza?" He didn't even wait for me to answer. "With *tomato paste*." He winked and patted my knee.

My heart squeezed in my chest as we crossed the parking lot and pushed through Ziggy's double doors. The restaurant was stuffed with people from church, all trying to squish into the tiny booths. It looked like every spot was taken, but then Miss O'Connor waved us over to her table.

"Hey, guys. Saved you a seat."

"How'd you know we were coming?" Dad asked.

"Lucky guess," she said, smiling. She pushed her thick glasses up on her nose.

Dad and Miss O'Connor chatted about the sermon and its various ties to the jungle reality show. I was only partially listening. When Dad got up to get a second plate of pizza, Miss O'Connor studied my face.

"What's wrong?"

"What? Nothing."

"Liar."

"It's nothing. Not a big deal. I don't really wanna talk about it."

"Hmm. Sounds serious."

"It's just . . ." I tried to think of how I could explain myself without telling her that my dad planned to ditch me for a stream of bachelorettes. "It's complicated."

She nodded until a pencil fell out of the messy bun on the top of her head. "Complicated. Yes. I get that."

"And . . . stuff is changing, and I don't like it."

"Change is hard." She took a bite of pizza and let a trail of cheese plop down her chin. "But sometimes it's good."

"Not this time."

She looked at me thoughtfully for a minute. "Well, you know what you can do? If all seems lost?"

I pictured the Delaware River on Christmas night in 1776. I was General George Washington, launching a surprise attack on the British.

"Gut 'em with your bayonet?"

Miss O'Connor smiled and widened her eyes behind her glasses. "I was going to say 'fight back,' but that's the general sentiment."

I nodded and, suddenly famished, shoved a too-hot bite of pizza into my mouth. *Fight back.* I could do that. I was smart and full of creative ideas for destruction. I knew what Dad needed, what Team Gravy needed. And it didn't involve stepmoms. Dad was about to experience the force of my full-scale resistance, and he had no idea it was coming.

4

Grocery Games

"What are these things called?" I asked, holding up a weird purple squash thing from the pile in the grocery store.

"That, my friend, is an eggplant. Nature's tasteless but colorful cousin of the potato."

"How do you eat it?"

Dad took the purple eggplant out of my hands and put it back on the pile. "You don't."

"You know, as my parental figure, you're actually supposed to encourage me to eat a variety of vegetables."

Dad turned to look at me, smirking. "Really?"

"Yup."

"Well, in that case, grab one of those bad boys, and we'll add it to our tacos."

I stood there, considering the offer for a second, my hand hovering above the shiny, smooth skin of the vegetables. But in the end, I remembered way too many of Dad's failed cooking attempts and decided it was best to play it safe. Nobody should mess with tacos.

"What else do we need?" Dad asked, scanning the super-market's freshest offerings.

"Well, we're out of pretty much everything."

"So we just need to go around and get one of every-thing?"

I shrugged.

Dad spotted the little shopping baskets at the end of the aisle and jogged over to pluck two from the stack.

"You're in charge of this half," he said, indicating the right side of the produce section, "and I'll get the other."

"Wait, what?"

"On your mark, get set, go!" Dad called over his shoul-der, already heading for the piles of apples on his side. "Remember, just one of everything! I want you to eat the rainbow!"

I laughed and started tossing stuff into my basket. One onion. One potato. One package of mushrooms that I scrunched my nose at. It wasn't looking much like a rain-bow so far.

Dad flew around the store, grabbing things so quickly he looked like a demented octopus. "I'm winning! I'm gonna wipe the floor with you!"

A lady with a kerchief tied over her curlers gave Dad a dirty look. He slowed down by a fraction.

"Hey, Grace. We'll need to make sure we knock before we open the fridge now. Know why?"

"Why?" I asked, flinging an orange into my basket.

"There could be a salad dressing!"

I chuckled. Sometimes his jokes are not far from funny. My basket weighed a million pounds, but I only had one more side of the display to nab. I bounced on my heels and threw things in willy-nilly. "Almost done!" I had no idea how we were going to fix all this stuff. And what do you do with one potato? I guessed we could split it. . . .

"Done!" Dad yelled, breezing past the curlers lady, who glared at him even more.

"I was done first!" I called, swinging my heavy load in front of his face.

"Let's call it a tie," he conceded.

"Or maybe we both lose, because this is a whole lot of vegetables we now have to figure out how to eat."

"Think of all the muscles we're going to get. You'll probably be able to bench-press a car after eating all these leafy greens."

"And you won't be able to leave the bathroom for days." I grinned at him as his face got a smidge redder. "Come on," I said, "let's venture to the cereal aisle. We're going to need some backup nutrition when we burn through all this."

But Dad didn't move. His eyes kept darting right over

my head at something that made his cheeks go pink and one corner of his mouth pull into a twitchy smile.

I turned, expecting to see a display of Dr Peppers shaped like Noah's ark (because what would be cooler than that?), but instead I saw a pretty dark-haired lady wearing sparkly diamond earrings like we were at a ball, not a grocery store.

I spun back to Dad, who was suddenly very interested in the contents of his basket.

"What is it? What's wrong? Do you know that lady?"

Dad shook his head and risked another glance at the woman. "No, I don't really know her."

"But you can't stop staring at her." The woman was inspecting cartons of strawberries.

"I'm not staring. I've talked to her a few times at church. I think her name is Rachel."

"Well, I don't know Rachel either, so can we please, please check out the cereal aisle?"

Dad raised his chin and hastily tucked his ABE LINCOLN IS MY HOMEBOY T-shirt into his jeans. "Uh, you go. I'm going to just talk to her for a sec. How's my hair?"

The words of the pushy ladies from church last Sunday buzzed in my brain. It was time for Dad to meet a nice young lady. Maybe this Rachel was a nice young lady. And he wanted to talk to her. Exchange eggplant recipes? And then ask her out! And he wasn't exactly asking my permission. He was asking about his hair. Which made me want to give him a noogie to mess it up.

I let out a long breath.

"Your hair looks . . . well, it looks messy, but I think it kinda works. I'll be over by the Cocoa Puffs."

I ducked around the nearest aisle and pressed my back against the canned goods. This was really happening. What could I do?

Suddenly my brain was flooded with the wise words of my history teacher: *Fight back.*

I peeked around the shelf and saw my dad. He shifted nervously from foot to foot, smiling like he'd just seen his first episode of *Jungle Survivor*. He was trying to help the woman select a ripe melon. Like he knew how to select a ripe melon. *Come on.*

Dad was laying it on thick, using all his charm. If this woman was super into dorky history-buff pastors, we were in real trouble.

He said something and the woman threw back her head in a too-loud laugh.

Uh-oh. He was pulling it off. She was picking up what Dad was putting down, and I felt my stomach clench as I watched them together. As soon as a potential love interest wandered into the area, I was completely off Dad's radar.

I looked around wildly, searching for anything that

might help me stop this madness. I could run screaming to my dad and say someone had tried to kidnap me. I could make sure the store manager saw me stuff candy in my jacket pocket. I could pretend to get stuck in a freezer in the frozen-foods section.

My eyes rested on a pyramid of creamed corn at the end of the aisle.

Perfect.

I skipped to the next aisle, found a cart, and threw in my basket of fruits and veggies. I started walking quickly toward the pyramid, the metal wheels jangling. The last few steps I jogged, just so I wouldn't chicken out. I had a feeling it was going to hurt, but adrenaline carried me through.

Crash! The noise echoed louder than I'd expected, and people from all over the store came to see what had happened. My dad and his lady friend were some of the first to arrive. It was like he remembered all of a sudden that he had a daughter. *Eye roll.*

"Grace! Oh my gosh, what happened?" Dad ran up to me, his eyebrows scrunched together, his T-shirt coming half untucked.

I smiled weakly at him. "Oops."

He reached out and touched my forehead, and I winced. "You're bleeding!" he said.

"I wasn't watching where I was going, I guess."

He stared at me, eyes narrowed, and then turned to the stock boy attempting to rebuild the pyramid and asked him to get me a Band-Aid.

Rachel patted Dad on the arm, said something too quietly for me to hear, and walked away with her melon. Dad didn't care, because he was so focused on me.

Mission accomplished. Soon enough the stock boy returned, offering a Dora Band-Aid, which Dad applied to my wound.

My head started to pound a little, so I was relieved when Dad grabbed the cart and pushed it, and me, toward the checkout line. All worth it to keep him from asking that woman out.

We paid for the stuff we'd selected. Dad promised to come back when I was at school the next day to finish the shopping, or else we'd have to become vegan.

We were quiet in the car on the way home. I tried to look innocent and slightly concussed so Dad wouldn't get mad at me. After all, as far as he knew, it was all an accident. A hailstorm of creamed corn could've happened to anyone, right?

He didn't ask me to carry a bag into the house, but I did anyway and even put the items in the correct drawers in the refrigerator.

"Hey, maybe we can play a game of Risk tonight?" I

asked. I wanted to get back to us just being us and remind him he didn't need anyone else to hang out with but me.

"You can't play Risk with brain damage," he said, tapping my Band-Aid and smirking at me.

"I'm feeling fine now, much better, really."

Dad's phone sat on the table, with a red dot that indicated a new voice mail.

"Oh, hey, someone called you." I played the message on speaker before Dad could protest.

"*Hi, Davy. This is Rachel, from the produce section. I mean, I don't live in the produce section, but that's where we were talking.*"

Dad scrambled to grab the phone, but I was quicker, ducking out of his reach. Rachel sounded almost as nervous as Dad had looked in the store. This was not a good sign.

"*I hope you don't mind, but I looked up your number in the directory because I felt like we were having a good conversation and then you had to leave so suddenly.*"

I glared at Dad. *Um, hello?* She didn't even ask if his daughter was okay after her run-in with a tower of cans.

"*I hope we can talk again, maybe over dinner on Saturday? My number is 555-1253. Hope to hear from you soon.*"

Dad yanked the phone out of my hand and jammed the button to shut off the message, but he had a big, dopey smile on his face. And it seemed, after all my hard work and vandalism, he had still gotten himself a date. *Rats.* My corn-canned forehead wound throbbed.

I'd taken a hit for Team Gravy, but I would really have to step up my sabotage game, or the next thing I knew Dad was gonna be taking this nice young lady to the movies.

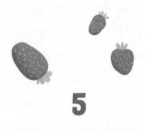

5

Plan of Action

I had a strategy session with Bea the very first chance I got, which happened to be at my house on Thursday night. Operation: Stepmom Shake-Up.

"Okay, here's the plan." I reached down to get a slobbery ball from Potus's mouth. "Dad is totally letting these church ladies bully him into doing something that is not only bad for him but bad for me. I have to make sure he doesn't go on any dates."

Bea scrunched up her nose. "How are you gonna do that? It's not like you can lock him in the basement."

I tossed the ball across the room, and Potus chased it. "I'm not ruling that out."

Bea pulled a package of Skittles out of her backpack and waggled her eyebrows at me. "Wanna taste the rainbow?" she asked.

I smiled. "Only half of it."

Bea dumped the candy out on the table and divided it up like we always do. Reds and greens for me. Purples and yellows for her. Neither of us really likes the orange ones, so those usually stay in the pile.

Potus jogged lazily back to me and dropped the ball at my feet, and I rewarded him with ear scratches. Bea gave me a look as I let him lick my hand and then shoved some Skittles into my mouth.

"Ew. That's disgusting." She shook her head at my germy hands, but there was a crooked smile on her face.

Bea has always been the type of person who has to do everything exactly right. I'm guessing that when her mom did her diapers, Bea undid them and rediapered herself to her own high standards. She doesn't give herself a lot of grace (ha, pun intended) when she's trying something new.

On our first day of kindergarten, the teacher demonstrated how to draw the letter A. All of us wiggly five-year-olds tried to copy the letter with our sharp new crayons. Bea sat at the yellow circle table with me, her lips moving quietly as she recited the directions the teacher had given us (up line, down line, cross it in the middle).

Bea was so tense, so worried she'd make a mistake, that her red crayon's tip snapped with the pressure. She burst into tears and told our teacher she didn't feel good and went to sit in the quiet corner.

I slapped my *A*s down in record time, using every crayon in my box and not caring in the slightest whether I stayed inside the faint lines of the paper. And then I skipped over to where Bea was sitting. She didn't look up at me; she was staring at her hands. I wiped my snotty nose on the back of my sleeve as I handed her my red crayon. "You can use my red. The end is still pointy."

Bea burst out laughing. "Don't wipe your snot on your arm! Use a tissue!"

I giggled and made a silly face at her. "I don't care. You wanna come back to yellow circle table? We can hold hands."

Bea smiled weakly and stood up. I extended my snot hand to her, but she grabbed the other one instead and we skipped back over to our table, best friends. Bea still likes to follow the rules, and I still like to break them, but somehow we're good for each other and make each other better.

I threw the ball for Potus again, but he'd lost interest. He just stared at me with a look that said, *I already got that for you once!*

"Hey, who are you gonna do your second-semester project on?" I asked. Miss O'Connor had assigned us an extensive research project on a famous American of our choice.

Bea's eyes lit up. "I'm doing mine on Jackie Robinson."

"Who was she?" I asked.

Bea laughed. "Not a she. Jackie Robinson was only the greatest baseball player who ever lived. Why are we friends again?"

I shrugged and we both laughed.

Bea put a purple Skittle in her mouth and chewed thoughtfully. "Let me guess. You're gonna pick one of your dusty old presidents."

"Duh. I'm going with Teddy Roosevelt, my favorite dusty president of the bunch."

"Don't you already know absolutely everything about him?" Bea smirked.

"There's always more to learn," I said. "And having a wide knowledge base will only make my report writing easier."

Bea shrugged. "You sound like your dad."

I scowled. My dad. Who was about to ditch me for a bunch of dates.

"What's wrong?" Bea asked.

"Dad and me. We spend all our time together. We have our projects and our history road trips and our documentaries. And if he's dating, he's not going to have time for all that. He's not going to have time for *me*."

Bea put her arm around me and squeezed tight. "Nothing could mess up Team Gravy," she said quietly.

"But what if it does?" My voice sounded high and squeaky. "I'm really worried. The other day, at the grocery store . . . he talked to a woman. Just walked right up and talked to her."

Bea tilted her head, her face sympathetic. "He's a pastor. He talks to a lot of women."

I huffed. "No. It was different. He liked her. And then she called him. And now they're going out to dinner."

I trailed off, my thoughts spinning wildly out of control. There had to be some way to fight back. I had to come up with a plan.

Bea recognized the look on my face. "What are you thinking?" she asked, a hint of apprehension in her voice.

"What if we make sure the dates he goes on . . . lack romance."

Bea scrunched her nose. "Translation?"

"Dad sets up the dates and we knock them down."

Bea pressed her lips into a thin line. I could tell she was thinking about all the rules we would have to break to commit sabotage. She let out a long sigh. "I don't know."

I pulled a notebook and pencil out of the junk drawer. "Just hear me out. I have a few ideas to run past you."

I wrote a dramatic number one at the top of the paper. "Let the air out of his truck tires."

Bea shook her head. "That's mean. Plus, what if you need a ride somewhere?"

"Okay, what about follow them to the restaurant and put dog chow in their food."

"Gross and also impossible. No restaurant is going to let you tamper with the food."

"I can set up a fake social media account for him where he is totally rude."

"That would probably get him fired."

"Indoor fireworks?"

"There is no such thing. And also dangerous."

I sighed. "You are such a downer."

"I am the voice of reason."

I wrote the number five and then tapped the eraser on the paper. "Hey," I said. "Remember that time when I made a big deal about seeing that ghosts-in-the-attic movie?"

Bea raised one eyebrow. "Yeah. You begged for weeks. Your dad didn't want you to see it."

"Yeah. He thought it would be too scary for me, but I strongly disagreed." I scooted the gross orange Skittles around on the table. "The thing was, my dad was kind of right. Once we got to the theater and the movie started, it was way too scary for me. I only made it through the first fifteen minutes and I had to get out of there."

"What? You never told me that! You said that movie was awesome!"

"I was embarrassed! It turns out that my nerves are not as sturdy as I thought they were. The point is, I had to fake a stomachache to get out of there."

Bea started to nod. "Okay, I see where you're going.

This could possibly work. You pretend to be sick so that your dad has to stay home. But if you get caught, I had nothing to do with this. My parents do not tolerate nonsense." She did a spot-on imitation of her mom, and we both laughed.

A little bit of the grocery store's stress left my body as I shoved the rest of my Skittles into my mouth. "Nonsense is my middle name," I said, rubbing my palms together.

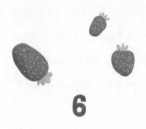

6

Fake It Till You Make It

On Friday night I couldn't sleep, so I spent some time reading my great-great-great-great-granny's diary and staring at the picture of her in the white lacy dress. It was a beautiful dress. My fingers itched to sew something like it. I Googled the 1904 St. Louis World's Fair and tried to imagine my dad and me walking through the amazing spectacle. Maybe I could get my picture taken right in the same place that Granny did. I drifted to sleep with pictures of carousels and parasols dancing in front of my eyelids.

Dad and I spent Saturday morning nosing through Springdale's only used-book store. They were having a sale, and the store was crowded, not with shoppers, but with additional tables loaded down with books. Outside the wind blew cold and blustery, and the windows of the store were frosted. We picked through dusty poetry books and outdated atlases, searching for anything related to American history. I was also looking for anything about clothes from 1904 because I could not stop thinking about Great-Granny's dress.

"Ah, the Father of Our Country!" Dad said, holding up a book with a chubby-cheeked, white-wigged George Washington staring down his nose at me from the cover. He looked ready for war, his eyes questioning me about my battle strategy. Dad's date with Rachel was tonight, and I had to put my plan into action.

I waited until Dad was on the other side of the store and then plugged my nose and held my breath. I could hold my breath an unreasonable amount of time until I got dark circles under my eyes. While I was not-breathing, I pulled a round container of blush out of my pocket and used my fingers to dab at my cheeks. Perfectly flushed.

Getting my dad to believe I was sick would be easy-peasy. He never really properly examines me. We don't even own a thermometer. If today was anything like my past attempts, he would give me medicine (the good-tasting kind), let me lounge on the couch, and baby me more than usual. *Sorry, Rachel!*

He wandered over to me, the George Washington book tucked under his arm.

"Hey! Find anything good?"

I let my eyes go glossy and unfocused and didn't answer him.

"Grace?"

"Oh, sorry, Dad. I guess I'm not feeling well." I would just stumble a bit on our way back to the truck, and BOOM, his date would be as good as canceled.

A look of concern passed over Dad's face, and I could see the wheels turning in his head. "You don't feel well?"

I nodded sadly and then pressed my fingers to my forehead to indicate that the motion caused waves of pain.

"She probably needs Tylenol and a nap." Miss O'Connor appeared out of nowhere, a stack of books in her arms and a smile on her face. She wore a polka-dot shirt and bib overalls. I didn't even know they made those for adults. Her glasses slipped halfway down her nose, and her hair created a halo of fuzz all around her head.

"Hi, Miss O'Connor," I said.

"Hey, there's where all the American history books went," Dad joked, touching the spines in her stack.

"You can borrow any you want," she said, readjusting the books in her arms. "I also got some vintage mechanics books. The fifty-seven Chevy I'm restoring is giving me fits."

I was losing my audience.

"Well, I'd better get home so you can give me some medicine and maybe make me some soup. From a can. No need to make a fuss." I tried to do my best impression of a flu victim, swaying a little bit and thinking nauseous thoughts.

"Oh. Yeah . . ." Dad took out his phone and started to scroll through. "I mean, I guess I can cancel my thing."

Miss O'Connor studied my face but turned to Dad. "What thing?"

"Oh, I had a . . . dinner . . . is all."

As bad luck would have it, Miss Marge, the Mrs. Claus look-alike from church, spied Dad and made a beeline. She put her hand on his arm and said, "Pastor Davy, I heard a rumor about you."

Dad raised his arms like he was surrendering. "It's all lies!"

Miss Marge giggled. "I heard you have a date with Rachel Watson. And I heard your daughter destroyed Gambly's Grocery Store." She gave me a narrow-eyed look, and I scowled.

Dad held the George Washington book like a shield, and his eyes flicked to Miss O'Connor. "Um, yes, Grace actually did destroy Gambly's. But it was an accident. And I guess the date part is true too."

"Hey!" I said, throwing my hands on my hips, but then remembered I was supposed to be sick, so I took them back off and coughed weakly. The church lady shuffled away, satisfied that she'd verified some juicy gossip.

Miss O'Connor cleared her throat. "I can take care of Grace for you while you go to your thing." She peered at me over her stack of books and winked. "I can give her

cod liver oil and tuck her into bed early and rub menthol on her feet and everything." I had the sudden feeling
that Miss O'Connor was onto me. It was like her years of
teaching middle school had turned her into a human lie
detector.

I wrinkled my nose. Cod liver oil and menthol did not
sound like fun. And it also didn't seem to be keeping Dad
from his date.

Dad stared. "Are you truly sick? I mean, sick enough
to cancel our plans?" *Our* plans? Sick enough to cancel on
Rachel is what he meant. He was more worried about can-
celing his dinner with some stranger than he was about his
sick child? *How rude.*

I had to consider my options. It didn't seem like he
would forget the whole date thing. So I was either stuck
with Miss O'Connor, pretending to be sick, or I could
wave the white flag.

I sighed. "I guess not. I'm probably just tired. Some
takeout and movies will revive me."

My history teacher grinned like a baby-kissing politi-
cian. "My, such a fast recovery. Have a great night, both
of you."

She smiled at my dad as she walked away, and he grinned
after her.

"So I guess we should go home," I muttered. "Maybe

I'll see if Bea wants to come over and keep me company."
Dad nodded and put his arm around me.

"Tell ya what. I'll buy you this very dusty George Washington book, since you're feeling bad. Deal?"

I shrugged but grabbed the book. "Deal." I needed to study up on war strategies, apparently.

Bea arrived right on time hauling a stack of teen magazines and a giant bag of Skittles. She bounced into the living room and plopped on the couch where I was "resting." Actually, I was pouting, but Dad didn't seem to be catching on.

"Hayley Mills or Lindsay Lohan?" she asked, kicking her sneakers up on the coffee table.

"Huh?"

"I thought we wanted to watch *The Parent Trap* for prank-spiration while your dad is on his date?"

"Oh. Right. I don't care—pick whatever you want." I knew my mind wouldn't be able to focus on anything other than my dad breaking up Team Gravy.

Dad sprinted downstairs wearing clean jeans and a button-down shirt. He had gel in his hair and he'd shaved, and it wasn't even Sunday.

"Well, girls, I hope I can trust you to stay out of trouble.

I'll be home early. Like by ten. Everything in Springdale is closed by ten, isn't it?"

The two of us are pretty much never out late on a Saturday night, so I had no answer for him.

"We'll be fine, Pastor Davy," Bea said.

"Have fun with the woman you hit on at the grocery store." I crossed my arms over my chest.

"What?" Dad spurted.

"Oh, sorry. Did she hit on you first?"

Bea's eyebrows shot up, and she watched us go back and forth like she was watching a tennis match. I was pretty sure she'd never witnessed me and my dad fight in the whole six years she'd been my friend.

"Nobody 'hit on' anybody, Grace. Geez, how do you even know that expression?"

I rolled my eyes.

"Will you two be all right here?" He stuck his chin out at me, daring me to tell him to stay home. I wanted to. I wanted to so very, very badly. There was no way Rachel-from-the-grocery-store could ever make us as happy as my mom had. My mind searched frantically for some stick of dynamite to throw at this situation, but I was coming up blank.

"Fine. Go on your ridiculous date. I hope you have a wonderful time and fly to Vegas to get married."

"Grace . . ."

I buried my face in a pillow while Bea walked him to the door. Dad pulled a crisp twenty out of his wallet and handed it to Bea for the pizza delivery. It was just the inspiration I needed.

I hopped up and gave my dad a quick and furious hug. It took him a second or so, but then he squeezed me back hard. He was so distracted by my light-speed mood change he didn't notice when I snuck his wallet out of his back pocket. He turned toward the door, and I tossed my prize on the couch before giving Dad one last wave.

And then he was gone, and my half of Team Gravy curdled.

"So I guess our plan was a dud?" Bea grabbed the remote from the table.

I smiled. "Operation: Stepmom Shake-Up is in full effect. Although somewhat delayed and not very well thought out."

Bea scratched her head. "Huh?"

I snatched up the wallet I'd tossed on the couch and waved it at her.

"I snagged this. Guess dinner is on Rachel." I chuckled at my own genius.

Bea shook her head as she ate a handful of purple and yellow Skittles. "That wasn't on the list."

I shrugged. "Sometimes you have to improvise."

While we watched the clueless twins prank each other

at camp, I told Bea about my failure to fake the flu in the bookstore.

Bea scratched Potus behind the ear. "But, you know, you could get a stepmom out of this whole thing. That could be kinda . . . nice."

"Stepmoms are never nice. Take the Cinderella story, for example. Plus, me and Dad have worked overtime to stay afloat after the accident. We don't need anyone messing up our system."

Bea nodded in agreement and gave me a big hug. "I know what you mean. Family situations can be so . . . wobbly."

I made a sound somewhere between a huff and a sigh. "Not your family."

Bea fiddled with the edge of the blanket that was wrapped around her knees.

"What's up?" I asked, losing all interest in the singing and dancing on the TV and studying Bea's face.

"My family is about to change. Big-time. I have a cousin, Julian, who's two. I've never actually met him because he and his mom live in California."

I wasn't sure where Bea was going with this, but I nodded to encourage her.

"I guess his mom got into some trouble. She's going to jail for a really long time. And she gave up parental rights to Julian. Family Services called us because we're his only other relatives, to see if we would consider adopting him."

Whoa. She wasn't kidding. That would be a huge change for sure.

"Well, what did your parents say?"

"They thought about it and asked me how I felt. . . ."

"How *do* you feel?" I asked, leaning closer.

"Honestly? Not great! I begged for a sibling for the first ten years of my life, and now that I'm over it and happy to be an only child, they're gonna adopt some screaming, pooping toddler. Plus, you know I'll get stuck taking care of him all the time."

I nodded. I couldn't imagine having a younger sibling either.

"But in the end, they said they would always regret it if they didn't step up and help the little guy in his time of need. He is family, after all."

"So he's coming to live with you? Like permanently?"

Bea nodded. "My only-child status expires next Friday."

I tried to imagine my life getting overturned like Bea's was about to be, and then a lump grew in my throat 'cause it was possible that it would. "I'm really sorry, Bea. I don't know what to say. That is just . . . unreasonable."

We hugged, and Bea sniffled a little bit, so I handed her a tissue.

"I can't help thinking that maybe . . . I'm not enough? You know? Like, why can't my parents just be happy with the one kid they have?"

I leaned over and put my head on her shoulder. "You are more than enough, Bea. Your parents are just trying to do the right thing."

Her voice was so quiet I almost didn't hear her say, "It doesn't feel like that."

I knew exactly what she meant.

7

Hammer Time

Dad and I spent all Sunday afternoon squishing itchy pink insulation between the studs of the attic walls.

"Are we done yet?" I grumped, adjusting my goggles as we pushed another big roll of the stuff up through the floor hatch.

"Oh come on. It's not so bad," Dad said, but then he started to itch furiously at his armpit and we both laughed.

I collapsed on the floor. "I want to get to the fun part. Power tools and paint."

"One step at a time, Giblet. We had to get the electrical all up to code so the house didn't go up in flames. And now we have to ensure that you don't freeze to death up here." His voice was muffled by the paper masks we had to wear to keep from breathing in the stuff.

"Minor details," I said. I was definitely more of a big-picture kind of person, while Dad liked to check each individual element off his to-do list. I liked the planning and dreaming about how it would all look when we were done, and he liked carefully completing each step. I helped him not get bogged down with the details, and he helped me not to skip steps.

It felt good to be spending an afternoon with Dad, just the two of us, like usual. I studied his face in the slanting attic light. He had dark circles under his eyes, and he seemed more distracted than usual.

I finally got up the nerve to ask him. "So, how did your date go last night?"

He sighed, pulling down his mask and pushing up his goggles. "Terrible." He rubbed his hand over his face and instantly realized he'd made an itchy mistake. He used the bottom of his shirt to try to undo it. "Would you believe I forgot my wallet?"

I avoided his eyes, suddenly very intent on holding up my rectangle of pink insulation.

"Oh wow. That's terrible. That must have really killed the mood," I said, trying to make my voice even.

"But honestly, the conversation wasn't going too well before that. She didn't even know which war Zachary Taylor fought in."

I snorted. "You talked about old Rough and Ready, huh?"

"Well, I mean . . . briefly. I didn't really know what to

say. You know, it's been a long time since I've been on a date."

I let the sad note of that last sentence slide over me, like I was wearing armor. I couldn't go feeling sorry for him now, or I'd quit my sabotage plans and Team Gravy would fall to pieces.

"So she wasn't into history trivia? Shocker."

"It wasn't only that. It was a lot of things. I tried to picture her here, with us, watching documentaries or eating burnt Pop-Tarts, and I just . . . couldn't. Plus she has a cat, and we are clearly dog people." Potus lifted his head off his paws and blinked sleepily at us.

Dad's face crumpled, and for a second, I felt terrible for stealing his wallet. I reached out and patted his arm, and a cloud of debris puffed off his flannel shirt, which made us both laugh, and then cough, and then laugh some more. The guilt melted away as tears of laughter, or maybe choking, ran down our faces. I would steal his wallet a million times if it meant he wouldn't go out with any more boring women he met in the produce section. Maybe things didn't have to change after all.

We worked in near silence for a few more minutes. Dad started humming a song from his favorite band, the Presidents. And that made me think of Teddy Roosevelt. And that made me remember the other thing I'd been working on.

"Hey, Dad," I said, giving my insulation a last shove

into place. "Did you know they re-create the World's Fair in St. Louis every year? They have vendor booths and rides and stuff, and it's in the same place they had it in 1904."

"Huh. Cool. What made you look into that?" Dad laid his piece flat on the floor so he could cut it to the right length.

"Great-Granny's journal. I think the building she stood in front of in the picture is the art museum. And it's still there! Wouldn't it be cool to get my picture in the very same spot?"

Dad looked up from his cutting and grinned. "Sounds like someone's planning a road trip!"

Dad and I have a bucket list of historically significant places we want to visit. Some of the best destinations are Mount Rushmore, Abe Lincoln's bronzed log cabin foundation, and the Upside-Down White House. There's even a statue of a billiken in St. Louis that's supposed to resemble President Taft (if he were part troll doll). We're going to rub its belly for luck.

I helped Dad haul up two more bundles of insulation.

"I've also been studying the fashion of the turn of the century," I said. "I need to get better at my sewing now that I'll have all this awesome space to set up my machine and dress form and stuff."

Dad nodded, and then his face lit up. "Hey, what do they call the guy who invented denim pants?"

"I have no idea," I said.

"A *jean*-ius."

"Good one, Dad." I grinned and shook my head. "But what would you think about a three-piece suit? There's a job at the World's Fare Heritage Festival I think we'd be perfect for."

He squinted. "Do they need me to baptize people in the fountain?"

"No. We could apply to be reenactors. They hire people to dress up like famous visitors from the original World's Fair in 1904."

"So I'd have to wear a suit, but I'd get paid."

"Yup. Just like every weekend."

"I'll think about it."

Which was as good as a yes.

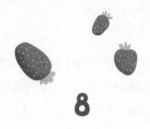

8

Growing Pains

I worried about Bea all week. She'd been quiet at school, but I'd tried to make her smile. I dropped a handful of purple and yellow Skittles into her hand whenever I got the chance. On Friday, Bea wasn't at school, and I knew it was because little Julian had arrived.

Saturday afternoon was cold and cloudy, so I bundled up to walk across the street to her house. I wanted to check on her and see how everything was going. As soon as my front door closed, I spotted her, shivering on our front porch, hugging her knees.

"Bea! What's wrong?" I asked, jogging over to where she sat and joining her on the steps. I put my arm around her shoulders and felt her trembling. My heart felt like it was being squeezed to bits.

"Everything." She shook her head, her eyes rimmed with red.

Bea was more of a crier than me, so it wasn't the first time I'd seen her sobbing, face dark like a thundercloud. But the fact that she was freezing on my front porch when she had a perfectly warm bedroom right across the street was new.

I had a sinking feeling why she might not want to go inside. "He's here now, isn't he?" I said, studying her face. "Tell me everything."

"Well, my mom had to get him from California. All Dad talked about while she was gone was how excited he was about Julian."

"That seems normal, though. You wouldn't want him to be unexcited, right?"

Bea shrugged and sniffed. "And then once Mom got back . . . it was like everything changed. My whole life was just dumped on its head. Julian has both of my parents wrapped around his little finger."

My nose was frozen and I couldn't feel my backside anymore, but I wanted Bea to keep talking. Maybe it would make her feel better to tell someone who cared.

"It's not how I thought it would be," Bea sniffed.

"How's that?" I asked.

"Well, I knew toddlers were a lot of work. And I was prepared to help. I read a book. I made lists. But what I didn't realize was that once Julian arrived, my parents would completely forget I exist." She smiled weakly. "Silly, huh?"

"But, Bea, I'm sure your parents appreciate your help," I offered.

She shook her head. "No. Not really. Since the minute he got here, they've barely noticed I'm alive. The few things I've tried to do to help have been wrong. I made a bath too hot, and I forgot to cut the grapes in half. My parents have been so busy." She gulped.

This was exactly what I knew would happen. Bea's parents got caught up in the new situation and left her out completely. Just like my dad would do to me if he got a new girlfriend.

When Bea first started playing the guitar, she was, like, obsessed. She would play all day every day. When I would invite her to come over or go to a movie or go play in the park, she'd say, "I can't right now. I have to practice." It had been rough for a while. I worried that I might lose my best friend to an instrument. But after a while the newness wore off, and Bea started showing up again—with gross calluses on her fingers, but still. I hoped this was like that. Maybe her parents were just obsessed with Julian because he was new. Maybe once they'd mastered the basics, they could find more time for Bea, just like she'd found her way back to me.

I tried to think of something to say to cheer my best friend up. "Things will probably settle down eventually.

And then your parents will realize what a big help you've been."

Bea's voice took on a high, strained tone. "They don't even know where I am right now! I just walked out the door and nobody even noticed or asked where I was going!"

Bea's parents *always* know where she is. They're kind of worriers and make her call if she goes anywhere besides school, church, or my house. It's not that they don't trust Bea, they say; it's that they don't trust the rest of the world.

One time we'd decided to go to a movie after church on a Sunday and Bea forgot to tell her mom. Halfway through the movie an usher with a flashlight and a very angry Mrs. Morrison interrupted the show. Bea was grounded for a week.

But on the whole, Bea's house is always a soft place for us to land. Her parents are kind and loving. They play board games and make hot cocoa. They show up for Bea's games and concerts and gymnastics competitions. Up until last night, Bea had been the center of their world.

I let out a breath that hung foggy in the cold air. "Well, I know where you are. You're right here with me." My head rested on her shoulder, and I gave her knee a squeeze. She sniffed again and leaned her head on me. We would lean on each other. And we wouldn't forget each other or replace each other. No matter what.

Dad stuck his head outside a few minutes later and told us to get our frozen rear ends inside. Bea and I didn't argue. My house felt warm and inviting after the shivery porch. Bea had finally stopped crying, and she reached for a cookie off the plate my dad put in front of her.

"I'm glad you're here, Bea," he said, smiling at her. "I wanted to ask you something. . . ."

Bea looked at him expectantly.

"What do you think of the beard?" Dad rubbed at his stubble. I had barely noticed it was there, and would most definitely not classify it as a beard just yet.

"It's nice, Pastor Davy," Bea said, trying to smile at him. He probably couldn't tell that her smile was fake, but I knew.

"I used to hate facial hair . . . but then it grew on me," Dad said, an evil glint in his eye. Bea and I both burst into giggles and I silently thanked Dad for his terrible joke, because it seemed to break the spell of sadness surrounding us.

I noticed that Dad had showered and was wearing real clothes, not sweatpants, on a Saturday. My palms went sweaty and my heartbeat went into triple time, but I tried to sound casual. "Where do you think you're going looking all fancy?" I asked, my voice sounding high and squeaky from panic.

Dad narrowed his eyes at me. "I'm meeting a friend."

"What friend?" I asked, narrowing my eyes back.

"A new friend. Zeke thinks we might hit it off." Zeke was the pastor of the Methodist church. He always wore a T-shirt in the swimming pool and had one of those nylon ropes to hold his glasses on.

"Are you serious right now? You're going on a blind date with someone Zeke-the-buzz-cut thinks you'll like?" I asked, standing up.

Dad sighed. "Grace, we've been over this. I'm dating now. I'm a guy who goes on dates." He sounded like he was trying to convince himself as much as me. "I won't be out late. We're going to Giovanni's."

"Bring us back some garlic knots, please," Bea said sweetly.

A dreamy look came over Dad's face. "Mmm . . . garlic knots. See, even if this date stinks, at least I get garlic knots." Dad kissed me on the head before he headed out the door.

I spun to face Bea, hands on my hips. "We are really gonna need to step it up, Bea! This is date number two. Nice work getting him to order the garlic knots. His breath will be rank at least. Now, what else can we do to guarantee this is a real train wreck?"

Bea scrunched up her mouth in her thinking face. "Are you sure you want to mess with him? I'm not convinced it's a good idea."

"Bea, you promised me your loyalty. I need you. This date has to go down in flames. We're gonna need some supplies."

"Fine, but no literal flames," she said.

"It just so happens that I've added a few ideas to our list." I didn't bother to get the notebook out, because I was pretty sure I could remember all my latest schemes.

"Number six, we give him poison ivy," I said, raising my eyebrows at Bea.

"There's a good chance that would backfire and we'd be the ones covered in calamine lotion. I am highly allergic," Bea said.

I went on, undeterred. "Fine. Number seven, we put hair remover in his hair gel."

"Whoa. Remind me not to get on your bad side. But I think you might regret that one. I mean, his hair could take months to grow back! Especially considering how wispy that beard was."

Sigh. "True. Okay, but number eight, do the same thing to his date's hair gel. Then she'd be the baldy."

Bea leaned forward. "There is no time for that! This date is happening right now. We need to think of something that we can do immediately to tank this dinner. Now think, you evil genius, you!"

A slow smile spread across my face. "I think you'll find that idea number nine will be right in the sweet spot. Not too heinous. But annoying and distracting."

"And nobody gets hurt?"

"Not a hair on their heads."

9

I Don't Wanna Be a Chicken

We climbed on our bikes and headed to Springdale's fanciest Italian restaurant, where my dad's truck was parked in the lot. Adrenaline pumped through my veins and escaped my body in the form of snickers. Bea kept glancing all around, with her head ducked and her coat hood pulled tight around her face. She shushed my giggles, and I tried to get serious as we crept up to the large plate glass window.

The dining room was packed with families and couples. It was dim inside, the tables lit by flickering candles on top of red-and-white-checked tablecloths. There were fake grapevines draped over all the ledges and archways, and accordion music floated out onto the street from the speakers. I squinted into the dimness, searching the faces for my dad.

"There he is," I said. "Far corner. Looks like she hasn't shown up yet." My dad sat ramrod straight, with a blank but pleasant expression on his face. He didn't glance at the menu or have his phone out, like most of the other diners did. He drummed his fingers on the tabletop.

"Maybe she won't show at all?" Bea offered hopefully.

"Or maybe she will, but she'll take one look at him and leave?" I added. This would be sad for my dad but would work out great for me. A victory without even putting up a fight.

Bea snorted. "Naw. Your dad is kinda cute. For an old-guy dad type."

"Gross."

"There she is!" Bea pressed her nose against the window as a woman came out of the bathroom and waved at Dad. Just then a waiter started to walk toward the empty table by the window to clean it off, and we had to duck. When we dared to peek again, Dad and the mystery lady were hugging hello.

"Whoa. She's pretty," Bea said, craning her neck for a better view. Dad's date had a short blond bob haircut and a red slouchy sweater. She was wearing white pants.

"I don't trust anyone who wears white pants. She's obviously uncomfortable with children," I whispered to Bea. "I mean, I'm a little old to be sticky all the time, but I still have been known to get wild with the ketchup and mustard." Bea nodded wisely.

Dad chatted about something, hand gesturing wildly, his ears and cheeks pink. What history anecdote or Bible story could possibly require all that flailing? They both laughed, and I felt my throat constrict. Time to get in there and shake things up.

I dug around in my backpack until I'd found my counter-move. It wasn't exactly fireworks, but it might cause enough confusion to derail their conversation at least. I stuffed my secret weapon under my shirt and whispered to Bea, "Let's get clucking."

My heart hammered in my chest, and my armpits went sweaty. I felt like I was a spy attempting to complete an impossible and dangerous mission. I would have to be stealthy. No one could see me, or I was d-e-a-d DEAD. Everyone in this town could pick the preacher's daughter out of a lineup. I waited by the back door until a busboy lugged a huge bag of trash to the dumpster, and then I slunk inside. Bea waited for me by the front window, watching my progress.

When I was close enough to see the nervous sweat on Dad's forehead, I took a deep breath to steady myself and pulled Clucky the Chicken out from under my shirt.

Clucky had been a gift on some long-ago birthday. Something I'd tried out once or twice but found too annoying, and so it had gone back on my shelf, never to be seen or thought of again. Until today. Today was Clucky's date with destiny.

I felt around his feathery backside until I found the

volume button and turned it from Mute to Max. I took one last look at Dad and White Pants, chatting over garlic knots, and jabbed the On button. "Clucky, if you pull this off, you can cross all the roads you want, and I promise never to question your motives!" Then I chucked the toy in a potted plant near their table and hightailed it out of there. It was basically like detonating a bomb.

Clucky erupted in a loud and quacky version of the chicken dance. People from all over the restaurant looked up from their spaghetti plates with confused and amused looks on their faces. Some covered their ears. Some started doing the hand motions to the chicken dance. I managed to slip out the back door and join up with Bea before anyone noticed me. She high-fived me, and we both dissolved in a puddle of silent giggles.

White Pants covered her ears. Dad tried to say something to her, but he was clearly not being heard. Between Clucky's song and the reactions of the other people in the restaurant, the volume had gone up in there by about a million decibels.

"Oh man, this is even better than I imagined!" I whispered to Bea.

Then there was silence, and I could picture the fuzzy chicken lying motionless at the bottom of the planter. Everyone in the restaurant looked around, still wondering where the obnoxious song had come from.

"Is that it?" Bea asked.

"Wait for it . . . ," I answered just as Clucky got his second wind and started up all over again.

"*I don't wanna be a chicken, I don't wanna be a duck, so I'll shake my butt!*" Clucky sang.

A baby started crying. The screeching kind of cry that makes people cringe. A big guy in a Hawaiian shirt stood up and danced along as if this was some sort of fun activity the restaurant was providing. A woman threw her napkin down and marched off to report the disturbance, like any of the restaurant staff weren't aware.

"Total chaos," Bea breathed. "You really have a gift."

My breath fogged up the window as I watched the bewilderment unfold. The dancing guy was a nice bonus I couldn't have predicted. But I still wasn't sure if the plan was working. I studied Dad's face. He looked confused. "I really, really hope he isn't remembering that his daughter has an annoying toy that sounds exactly like this audio assault," I whispered.

"He looks way too flustered to be connecting those dots. For all he knows, you're at home with me, watching TV and pigging out on junk food," Bea replied. Dad's face fell, and I wondered if he thought his dates were cursed. First the forgotten wallet, and now this disaster. Good. Maybe he'd stop going on them.

It took a waiter two minutes and forty-five seconds to

locate the chicken in the plant and turn it off. (Bea was timing on her watch.) The crowd erupted in applause, and Hawaiian Shirt Guy wiggled his butt one last time for good measure.

White Pants did not seem amused. She took a long drink and then pulled her phone out of her purse. I saw Dad flinch. He hated technology in general, but phones at the dinner table were a major no-no.

"Things are definitely going south," I said, and Bea nodded.

Dad tried to ask a few questions. Or maybe he was just telling terrible jokes? But either way, after a few minutes he pulled his own phone out of his pocket.

Success. I didn't know if we had done enough, but it was all we could do for now.

"Retreat!" I called to Bea, grabbing my bike from the bushes. We zipped through the chilly night air, pumping our legs to the rhythm of the chicken dance.

10

My Girl, Alice

The next Friday, Bea and I snuck Skittles under the table in Miss O'Connor's history class. We were working on our famous-Americans project, and I couldn't help but be fascinated by Mr. Teddy Roosevelt, *the* most interesting president our country has ever had. The room buzzed as people worked in small groups, sharing the information we'd uncovered.

Bea accepted a purple Skittle and covertly ate it without lifting her eyes from her book. I studied her for a second, temporarily distracted from my reading. Her blond pigtails were fuzzy, her clothes wrinkled. She had dark purple dents under her eyes, and her cheekbones looked especially sharp.

"Are you okay?" I whispered.

Bea leaned toward me and whispered, "Having a toddler in the house is bonkers. BANANAS. Julian is into EVERYTHING."

I tried to think about what that might mean, but I had virtually no experience with toddlers, so I was drawing a blank.

She continued. "He climbed up onto his steppy stool and dumped an entire bottle of bleach into the washing machine." She held out her purple shirt, which was now splattered with white spots that looked a bit like pigeon poop.

I tried not to laugh, but I must not have done a great job, because Bea punched me in the arm and Miss O'Connor had to shush us. "It's not funny!" Bea's soft voice wobbled. "We baby-proofed the entire house. We put locks on all the lower cabinets. The bleach had a childproof cap, and it was on a really high shelf. I mean, he was only out of my sight for like ten seconds! He's a mini-tornado of destruction! Look at my library books!"

Her pile of Jackie Robinson biographies looked normal from the outside. Maybe the corners were mushy, like they'd been chewed. But then she started to flip through them and almost every page was colored on or ripped.

"Oh, snap," I said softly.

"I have *never* had to pay the library for damage before. Never." She pulled a particularly rumpled paperback out of the stack and waved it in my face. "He tried to flush this one down the toilet! He was supposed to be napping! Does that seem like napping to you?"

I wasn't sure if I was supposed to answer that.

Bea's eyes filled with tears. "This will cost me my entire savings account." She wiped at her cheeks angrily.

This was exactly why you should leave families well enough alone! I mean, weren't me and Dad doing all right by ourselves? What if adding another person completely ruined everything, like Julian had done to Bea's family?

We flipped through our books, commenting every once in a while on things we wanted to add to our reports. I was distracted, though, by Bea's troubles. I hoped they wouldn't soon become my troubles.

Then a sentence from the Roosevelt biography I was reading snagged my eye. "Hey," I said to Bea, who was still sniffling. "How did I never know this before?"

Bea looked up. "What?"

I leaned closer to the thick book. "Teddy Roosevelt had a daughter, Alice."

Bea scoffed. "Even I knew that."

"That wasn't the part I didn't know. His wife, Alice's mother . . . died."

Bea bit the end of her pencil. "That's sad."

"She died within days of Teddy's own mother. Listen to this quote. . . . *Sometimes when I realize my loss I feel as if I should go wild.*" The words squeezed something close to my heart. Teddy lost his mother and his wife all at once. I could understand the feeling of being wild with pain.

I glanced over at Miss O'Connor, who was helping another student, and then tapped my book with my pencil. "How come my dad never mentioned this? It's like . . . so major? Alice Roosevelt lost her mom just like I lost my mom!"

Bea put her hand on my sleeve. "Maybe that's why he never mentioned it. I mean, it's not like he talks about your mom very often."

I gulped and nodded, staring at the picture of Alice as a little girl. We were in the same club, me and her. The Dead Mom Club. And I instantly felt like I knew her better than I even knew Bea. We had this same terrible thing in common and it made us like sisters, even though we lived a lifetime apart. And I knew that if we were ever sitting across from each other, face to face, she would know what it was like to be on a team of two.

Dad has the best laugh. I mean, sure, he's usually cracking up at his own jokes, but it's a really great sound. And he has these big, rough hands that seem like they could catch me no matter what. He still says my prayers with me at night and tucks me in, even though I'm probably too old for that. He always tells me that if he could pick any girl in the whole world to be his daughter, he would still pick me.

I had been the center of his world for a long time now. And I wasn't ready to give that up.

A black-and-white picture filled one page of the book.

"It looks like Alice's father didn't stay single for long. He remarried and then had a *bunch* of kids."

"Alice had little siblings?" Bea craned her neck, suddenly a lot more interested in my book.

"Yup. Five of them. Four half brothers and a half sister. Can you imagine that?"

Bea shook her head. "Five times the chaos that is currently at my house? No thank you."

Miss O'Connor walked over and smiled at my notes. "I see you've discovered more than a few interesting facts about our twenty-sixth president."

I nodded, my head still churning up the information of Teddy and Alice's blended family.

Miss O'Connor leaned in, like she was telling me a secret. "Did you know one of his sons was named Kermit? Like the frog."

I giggled and the bag of Skittles crinkled in my lap. Miss O'Connor raised one eyebrow at me but meandered over to the next table. She really was the coolest teacher.

Bea sighed and leaned closer to her book. "This either says Jackie Robinson was named Rookie of the Year or Cookie of the Year. The print is completely smeared."

"I'm no baseball expert, but Cookie of the Year doesn't sound like a real thing." I slid her three purple Skittles plus two of my reds because sometimes you gotta share your rainbow with the people you love the most.

11

On the Rebound

Dad had been moping around the house ever since his disas-
trous chicken dance date, and the box of garlic knots he'd
brought home never got eaten. He seemed to be checking
his phone a little more than usual, but as far as I knew,
White Pants hadn't asked for another date, and neither had
he, so we were in the clear.

I made pancakes for dinner on Wednesday night, and
Dad got a smidge happier when I fried up some bacon to go
with it. We sat at the kitchen table munching on flapjacks
and not talking much until Dad cleared his throat.

"This weekend . . . I have a . . . there's this . . ." He almost choked on his words, searching my face frantically for
some sign of recognition.

"What? What is it? Do you have another setup?" I
tried not to spit the words, but despite the syrup they
tasted sour.

"No. The Missions Committee does this fundraiser every year. . . ."

I blew a raspberry, flicking bits of pancake into my bangs. Not a date. A church fundraiser. Why was he acting so weird about it?

". . . The First Baptist Bachelors and Baskets auction."

The words hung in the air as I tried to swallow my bite of food. Bachelors and Baskets auction? It sounded slightly familiar. I was pretty sure I'd never gone before. Why would I? Because that was where you went to *buy* a date with a man.

"Are you volunteering at the auction? Collecting money or organizing the event or something?" *Please say yes, please say yes, please say yes.*

"Or something. Miss Donna, from the Building and Grounds Committee, suggested I participate. So I could meet a nice young lady." Dad rolled his eyes and tried to win me over with a charming smile, but I knew what that "or something" would be. He'd be auctioned off to whoever would pay the most to share a picnic basket with Pastor Davy.

"Ew, Dad, no!" I threw my fork down in disgust, and Potus lifted his head from his paws, ears perked up at the possibility of falling food. "That auction will be gross! It will be old ladies waving their number cards in the air and whispering behind their hands about which man is the best catch!"

Dad lifted his chin, ever so slightly. "Well, I'm a good catch."

I groaned. "Dad. Just because you're all gung ho for meeting Miss Right doesn't mean you have to sell yourself out like this."

Dad picked at his pancakes. "Grace, I know you aren't exactly excited about me going on dates." His voice softened. "But you should know that I could never, ever in a million years replace your mom."

I gulped. I wanted to tell him that it wasn't Mom I was worried about him replacing. It was me. What if he found someone he wanted to spend time with more than his own daughter? I wanted to tell him he was threatening Team Gravy every time he went on another date. But the words stuck in my throat like they were covered in pancake syrup.

Dad patted my shoulder. "Hey, maybe someone awesome will bid on me. I could raise a bunch of money for the missions team *and* end up with a perfectly pleasant date for the evening."

I exhaled sharply but tried to make my voice firm. "Or someone terrible could bid on you and you'll eat your picnic basket staring at her chin hair while she talks about her teacup collection!"

Dad laughed. "It's all for fun anyway. And it's a good cause. I'll look at it that way."

All for fun. Good cause. I repeated the words in my brain on an endless loop.

I stood up so fast my chair nearly toppled over. "Can I borrow your phone? I need to text Bea."

Dad nodded, digging his phone out of his pocket while watching my face a little too closely. I wasn't gonna just sit back and let him be sold to the highest bidder, and then let that person wiggle her way into our family. I hoped Bea didn't have any plans this weekend, 'cause I needed her to help me brainstorm. I had to blow up this whole basket date, and fast.

12

A Power-Packed Picnic

Each of the bachelors of the Bachelors and Baskets fund-raiser had to provide a picnic to share with the winner of their date. Most of the men brought fried chicken or a cold pasta salad, but my dad was exceptionally ungifted at cooking. He happily packed two peanut butter and jelly sandwiches, some chips, apples, and cookies as his offering. It looked like what a second grader would pack in a lunch box, and not at all romantic.

He had carefully wrapped the sandwiches in waxed paper and tucked everything inside the wicker basket. He hummed while he added two paper napkins and two cans of soda.

"Hey, Grace," he said. "Why did the swimmers put peanut butter in the sea?"

I smirked. "I dunno, Dad. You tell me."

"To go with the jellyfish." He winked at me and smeared a blob of peanut butter on my nose.

"Hardee har har," I said, aiming a spoonful of jelly at his face, but he ducked, just in the nick of time, and it plopped onto the floor instead. We giggled as we cleaned up the smears, and I couldn't help but think that I had the most fun dad of all the dads. And what would happen if he fell for some uptight lady who didn't allow peanut butter and jelly fights in the kitchen? Or what if they only wanted to throw peanut butter and jelly at each other and they told me to get lost? Who would I launch jelly at then? WHO?

And then he left the basket sitting all alone on the counter while he went to run errands before the fundraiser. Mistake. Big mistake.

I messaged Bea from my computer and paced the kitchen, casting furtive glances at the picnic basket and wringing my hands like a cartoon villain.

After what seemed like an eternity, Bea burst through the back door into the kitchen. "I'm here. Ready for action. What's the plan?"

I pointed at the basket. "That."

She looked at me with her head cocked to the side. "I'm going to need some more information."

I sighed. "Dad is going to a fundraiser at church tonight, and he has to bring a picnic basket to share with some lady."

"So?" Bea said, sitting down at the table and helping herself to an orange.

"So, it's a date. I mean, it's just a picnic at church, but still, I don't want him to go falling in love over peanut butter and jelly."

Bea wrinkled up her nose. "Is that what he packed?"

I nodded. "Yeah, but I think we can do better. Or worse. Depending on how you look at it." I walked over to the basket sitting on the counter and dumped its contents theatrically in the trash. And then I reached in there and fished it all back out, 'cause I wasn't going to waste perfectly good food. I opened one of the bags of chips and took a loud, crunchy bite.

But I left the basket empty and gestured to it dramatically. "In this basket, we are going to put all of the most disgusting date foods of all time. Foods that are messy. Foods that are stinky. Foods that make you fart. I will prepare the world's most unromantic picnic, and you are going to help me."

Potus wandered into the kitchen and lay at Bea's feet while she reached down and scratched him behind the ears. "And your dad has no idea we're doing this?" she asked, avoiding my eyes.

"Does my dad know we're planning to sabotage yet another date? No. No, he doesn't."

Bea shifted on her seat. "But it's not even really a date. Like, there's a good chance he won't even like whoever buys him."

"That's not the point, Bea. Love can blossom at any time. I saw that in a jewelry commercial one time."

"I don't like it. I honestly can't believe you haven't gotten caught yet. Maybe we should just leave your poor dad alone."

"Did I ever tell you about the time my dad had a cavity but refused to go to the dentist?" I opened the refrigerator and started stacking ingredients in my arms. "He walked around the house moaning and putting ice packs on his cheek and only chewing on one side of his mouth for days. But he has this thing about the dentist, so he refused to make an appointment."

"So what happened?" Bea asked, wrinkling her nose. She was probably very put out by someone not going to the dentist. She goes every six months and is still in the no-cavity club.

"I told him I needed him to drive me to the hair salon. The one that's right next to the dentist's office in the strip mall. He, of course, didn't pay any attention to what door we walked into. And when I signed him in, he was right on time for his appointment. He was mad for like ten seconds, but since we were already there and he didn't have a lot of time to get scared, he got his tooth fixed."

I spread all the grossest contents of the refrigerator out on the counter and started taking inventory. "Just like the dentist, this is for his own good. We're doing this so my dad

doesn't have to suffer through the pain of a terrible relation-
ship, much like a rotting, disgusting cavity. We really have
no choice but deception if we want to save Team Gravy."

Bea sighed. "Fine. What do you need me to do?"

Bea rode with us to the auction because she couldn't wait
to watch Dad "strut his stuff" down the catwalk. Okay,
there wasn't really a catwalk. Only the red-carpeted stage
in the sanctuary of the church, but it would still be pretty
hilarious.

When we pulled into the church parking lot, Dad killed
the engine and sat there, staring into space. "This is okay.
I'm okay. Let's do this," he said.

Wait, he wasn't nervous, was he? 'Cause this was all his
terrible idea.

He marched into the church with his head held high—
Bea and I trailing behind him—to be sold like a lumpy used
mattress to the highest bidder.

The sanctuary pulsed with bodies, steamy hot compared
to the crisp snowy outside temperature. Old-lady perfume
wafted through the air and the sound of a gaggle of grand-
mas filled the large space.

It was a sea of white heads and cardigans.

Dad stood frozen in the doorway.

My heart leapt with joy because, let's face it, the prospects here weren't looking too good.

I grabbed his hand and dragged him up on the stage, where the rest of the bachelors were seated, waiting for the event to kick off. Miss Donna wore a pink pantsuit and carried a clipboard. She walked from bachelor to bachelor, checking facts on their bios and making sure they were in the right order. Her face lit up when she saw my dad trailing behind me.

"Pastor Davy! We're so *honored* you've volunteered to help us raise some money tonight! And *my*, don't you look *wonderful!*" she cooed, squeezing his bicep. My dad squirmed under her fingers. "Here's your seat, right here. Just wait until I call your name; then walk to the taped X at the front of the stage and stand there until someone wins you."

I elbowed Dad in the ribs. "*If* someone wins you."

He scowled, and I felt a tiny flicker of guilt because he was sweaty nervous about the whole thing.

Miss Donna tapped her clipboard. "Did you bring your basket?"

I smiled and held the wicker picnic basket up to her.

"I almost forgot that on the counter," he said, taking the handle from me. "Thanks for remembering." He squeezed me into his armpit and kissed the top of my head. "Team Gravy for the win."

A ten-pound bucket of guilt knocked me in the guts. "Don't thank me yet," I muttered as I hurried down the stairs and found my spot next to Bea.

The women got quiet as soon as Miss Donna walked up to the microphone. "Good evening, ladies of First Baptist! Thank you for braving the snow to come out tonight! We at the Missions Committee hold this event annually to raise money for our adopted missionaries in Africa and Europe."

The ladies bobbed their heads and murmured approval.

Miss Donna went on. "Remember, if you'd like to share a picnic dinner with the eligible bachelor on the stage, simply wave your number sign. Flourishing said sign is an agreement to pay the stated amount. Let's give it a try, shall we?"

The women obediently fluttered their little round number signs in the air and then giggled for some reason. It didn't look all that fun to me.

Bea leaned over and whispered in my ear, "Your dad looks like he's about to puke."

If he felt like puking now, just wait until he saw what we'd packed in that basket.

"Excellent. Let's kick off the auction with a wonderful bachelor. Not only is he the head of the Springdale Chess Club, but he works right here at the church as a custodial engineer. Do we have twenty-five dollars for Ed Smalley?"

One lady in the front tentatively raised her number.

Ed blushed all the way to the top of his bald head.

"Thirty-five?"

Another paddle.

Ed ended up being escorted off the stage by a fluffy-haired granny in a floral dress for the grand total of fifty dollars.

Dad looked a whole lot more cheerful.

I'm sure he thought if old Ed could sell for fifty bucks, the young and handsome pastor would sell for even more.

When Dad's turn finally came, Bea and I snickered behind our hands as Miss Donna read his bio. "Ladies, we have an incredibly special bachelor up next. You know him as Pastor Davy, shepherd of this very flock. He enjoys reading, studying, and long walks . . . among the cow patties?" She looked at Dad quizzically. His eyes widened and his nostrils flared. I'd made a few minor changes to his write-up before we left the house.

"He's looking for a woman who can bench-press more than him and disagrees with all his political views."

He started shaking his head then, looking for an opportunity to interrupt, but Miss Donna plowed on.

"Let's start the bidding at fifty. I see your fifty. How about seventy-five? I see seventy-five. One hundred? I see one hundred. One fifty? I see one fifty. Two fifty?"

Dad looked wide-eyed and pale as paddles flapped all over the sanctuary. A pause swelled after two fifty, but one lone paddle poked its way above the sea of heads. "*Sold* for two hundred and fifty dollars to Miss Regina Wrangler."

Miss Regina. The name sent a chill down my spine. She'd finally won the pastor's attention for a mere two hundred and fifty dollars. I watched the back of her poofy yellow hair as she marched up to the stage to claim her prize, and my hands curled into fists.

Three years earlier, eight-year-old me stood in the middle of the kitchen, staring at the mess.

Knock, knock.

If Mom were alive, she would've dropped dead all over again before answering the door with our kitchen in this state. There were takeout boxes, crumby casserole dishes, and brown banana peels covering every square inch of the blue Formica countertop. A rotten sweet smell drifted from the overpiled garbage, and my socked foot stuck to a brown puddle on my way to the back door.

I paused, my hand on the knob, and peered through the sheer curtains blurring the crisscrossed panes of the window. I sucked in a deep breath as I recognized the unexpected visitor. Miss Regina stood in the bright afternoon sunshine, her yellow hair pulled up into a bun on the top of her head. She carried a foil-covered glass dish.

Not again. No more. Why can't everyone just leave us alone?

I thought about trying to make a run for it, to crawl across the sticky floor so the widow couldn't see me, and hide under my bed until she went away.

But she wouldn't.

She'd stand there, knocking and knocking, and I was the only person who'd bother to answer.

I puffed out a breath and tried to arrange my face so it looked blank, bored, and uninterested in Miss Regina and her stupid casserole.

"Grace! How nice to see you, dear! Might I come in?" She pushed her shoulder against the door, her hips squashing past me. Her high-heeled shoes stuck to the black-and-white-checked floor.

I didn't know what to say, so I said nothing as she tiptoed through the kitchen and swung open the refrigerator, trying to find a home for the dish. Her eyebrows pinched together at the stacks and stacks of unheated dinners that left no room for her offering. She finally turned on her heels and placed it on top of the stove.

"Looks like this will just have to be dinner for tonight! It's my famous lasagna recipe. Lots of extra cheese."

I choked on the words *thank you.* My mom had made the best lasagna anyone had ever tasted. I forced my mouth into a smile and silently vowed that the pasta would be added to the mountain of garbage as soon as she was gone.

Something in her face shifted. "How are you holding up?"

It was the question of the day. Of the week. Of the last three months. The question drifting through everyone's mind in our small town. How were the young minister and his poor daughter holding up since the tragic death of their beautiful wife and mother?

"Fine," I said, the lie aching in my belly like churning acid.

Pity touched the widow's eyes as she crossed the kitchen to put her hand on my shoulder. I ducked out from under her touch.

"That the truth?" she asked, not unkindly.

The truth was we were bloated fish corpses in a moss-covered pond. We were crumpled-up plastic bags drifting across the Walmart parking lot. We were dirty, flea-ridden kittens dumped in a box on the side of the road.

"Course it's the truth."

"Where's your daddy?" she asked, the lipsticked smile reappearing. "We've missed him at church of late." She tried to look over my shoulder to the untidy living room, but I knew she wouldn't spot him there. He hadn't left his bedroom in a few days. He hadn't left our house in weeks.

He hadn't said my bedtime prayers with me since it happened. There was no way he'd come out for a social call with some pushy single lady from church.

"He's not feeling well. Might have a cold or something." I opened the door so maybe she'd get the hint and take her backside out the way she came.

"Oh! Maybe I'll stop by later with some chicken noodle soup. I remember well the tragedy of losing my own Harold. I'd like to be there for your family in this time of need."

"We aren't a family anymore." The words trickled out of my mouth without my permission and slammed on the sticky floor, bouncing off the walls and ceiling.

"Like heck we aren't."

Only he didn't say *heck*.

Dad appeared in the doorway to the living room, rumpled and pajamaed but awake. He looked angry. And he'd said a swear, which meant a dollar in the jar.

He marched over to the stove and gripped the edge of the casserole dish with white knuckles before thrusting it at Miss Regina.

"Grace and I will be just fine, Regina. Please spread the word that we'll no longer be accepting casseroles, meatloaves, soups, or stews. My daughter and I have everything we need."

The words bashed me in the rib cage. *We'll be fine. We have everything we need.* How could that be true when Dad seemed out of his mind with grief and I felt hollow and empty? Could the two of us really be everything the other needed?

Miss Regina's neck had gone a bit pink. Her trembling fingers held the lasagna as a sort of shield between her and Dad.

"Well, I'll surely spread the word, Pastor. Glad to hear all is right and the two of you are doing okay."

"We're doing more than okay. Or at least . . ." He paused and searched my face. "Or at least we will be. Me and Grace, we're a team. All we need is each other."

We're a team. Me and Dad. And he'd said we would be just fine, and he had never ever lied to me in all my eight years. He had crossed the room and hugged me so hard I felt all the doubt squeeze out of me. I'd believed him, with every cell in my body.

And now he was going on a romantic picnic with this very same casserole-pushing woman.

13

Fire at Will

Bea smacked me in the arm, and I shook my head to bring myself back to the present. "They're heading downstairs," she said. I watched as Miss Regina slid her arm through my dad's. Her face looked radiant with excitement. His looked a little bit green around the edges. Something told me this was not quite the outcome he'd hoped for, and I felt a smidge relieved.

Miss Regina chattered nonstop, and Dad smiled tensely and nodded. I bet he was wishing he was sitting on the couch with me, watching *Jungle Survivor* in our pajamas. That's what he got for messing with the team.

"Come on, let's go," Bea said. We were supposed to walk home after the auction, 'cause no kids allowed for the date portion of the evening.

"Hey, you know what we should do?" I had to choose my words carefully or Bea would put up a fight. She narrowed her eyes at me, and I continued. "We could sneak down to the basement and just watch how the dates go. I mean, it will be hilarious. Everyone will be all nervous and weird around each other. We can hide somewhere and watch the whole thing like a terrible TV show."

"Kids are not allowed. Plus, you'd be spying on your dad," Bea said dryly.

I shrugged. "It could be fun?"

Bea looked thoughtful and then linked her arm through mine. "I don't know how you always manage to talk me into these things, but I'll admit, I want to see what happens when he unpacks that basket."

"Me too. Come on," I said.

We took the back set of stairs to the community room in the basement. A few of the lucky couples had already arrived and stood there awkwardly chitchatting while holding their baskets. Red-and-white-checked tablecloths were spread all over the floor, and shiny foil hearts hung from the ceiling. I spotted a beverage table in one corner, covered in a floor-length tablecloth. Bea and I snuck over and crawled underneath. It smelled like old gum under there, but there was a seam at the corner that gave us an excellent view of the room. As long as our targets got a spot close to the drinks, we'd be able to see everything. Well, one of us would. We had to take turns peering out the crack.

The rest of the couples slowly filled the community

room, and I was the first to spy Dad and his date. Miss Regina had to be at least fifty, but she kept her hair dyed a yellowy blond. She wore stylish clothes, and I don't think I'd ever seen her without super-high heels. But she always had lipstick on her teeth, and she smelled like an old couch. I suspected she kept hard candy in her purse.

Luckily for us, they took a spot not too far from the beverage table. Unluckily for us, every time someone came up to get a glass of iced tea, our view got blocked.

As a pair of corduroy pants finally moved away from the drinks, I got my first glimpse of Dad. He clutched the basket tightly, a hopeful grin on his goofy face. I started to feel kind of bad about the shenanigans that were about to unfold. But then I remembered that fierce hug Dad had given me all those years ago, and how he'd promised we were a complete set, just the two of us, and I felt my guilt trade places with anger. What had changed? What had made him go from "My daughter and I have everything we need" to "Why, yes, Miss Regina, I would like to share my peanut butter and jelly with you." It made no sense.

Somebody turned on a CD of classical music, I guess to give the place a more romantic vibe, but it also made it impossible to hear what people were saying. I let Bea have a turn as lookout as I hugged my knees to my chest under the table.

Bea pressed her eyeball to the sneaky spy seam. "Your dad is unpacking the food. His face is the color of oatmeal. That doesn't seem healthy. I can't hear him. Oh, he's pulling out the chili."

I giggled into my hand and Bea swatted at me. "He's desperately searching for his peanut butter and jelly."

"Instead he will find baked beans. And prunes. And asparagus."

"You're wicked, you know that? You basically packed fart juice."

I scooted over to the crack. "Lemme have a turn. I'll be able to tell when my plan starts to work."

We swapped places and Bea lay on her back. "Remind me not to let you ever pack a romantic picnic basket for me. Like ever. In fact, I don't even want you cooking for me."

"Trust me, no one wants that. My chili might actually kill someone."

The person who'd been getting a drink finally returned to their spot and I had my first clear view of Dad and Miss Regina. She sat very straight and proper, her knees off to one side and her skirt spread around her like a cupcake wrapper.

Dad sat as far as possible from her on the blanket, criss-cross applesauce so he could lean away if he needed to. He'd placed the basket in the middle and had all my goodies spread out around them. The widow nibbled on corn on the cob, which I hoped would get disgustingly stuck between her teeth. Dad scooped chili out of the thermos onto the paper plates I'd packed.

Here's the thing about my dad. He can't resist the things he knows are bad news. Every single time he eats this stuff, he spends the rest of the night being miserable, but he can never say no. I saw the concern etched on his face as he ate a spoonful of the spicy chili and then tried to answer a question with his mouth full. Not a good look.

"What's happening? Are they kissing?"

"Ew. No. Dad's stuffing his face with ammunition, so he'll soon be prepared to fire at will."

"You have a dark gift," Bea said.

Miss Regina was now trying to eat the spaghetti I packed extra ladylike. But there comes a point in every spaghetti-eating experience when one simply must slurp. And don't believe the cartoons. Nobody wants to share the slobbery other end of the noodle with you, *Lady and the Tramp*–style. Dad cringed when she slurped the noodle and the saucy end came up and hit her in the eye.

Bea took her turn as spy and watched for a few minutes while I kicked back. She reported, "Well, I'd say Miss Regina is officially unkissable. She's got sauce all over her face and corn in her teeth, and since we added lots of extra onions and garlic to that spaghetti, I'm guessing her breath is nasty." We high-fived.

The next time I got a clear look at them, Dad had finished his food, but he'd also switched positions on the blanket. He leaned on his elbows, away from Miss Regina, presumably to let his stomach stretch out. I was glad to see he hadn't unbuttoned his pants, like he often did at home when his gut bulged full of gas. His date talked and laughed and attempted to get him to join in, but he stayed very quiet. At least his mouth did.

"Your poor dad. I know we're trying to protect Team Gravy, but it stinks to have to hurt him in the process."

I squirmed uncomfortably. "I know. I do feel a teeny bit guilty. But Dad has always said that me and him are just fine the way we are. So why does he all of a sudden wanna add someone else to the mix?"

"All right, my turn, then. Move over." Bea pressed her eye to the crack in the tablecloth and gasped.

"Oh my gosh. People are actually moving away from him. There's an invisible cloud of farts surrounding him now, and people are glaring at him and scooting away."

I smiled and lay with my hands behind my head like a pillow. "Exactly how I planned it."

The music stopped and the crowd turned to pantsuit-wearing Miss Donna, who made some sort of announcement about how much money they'd raised for the Missions Committee. In a moment of silence, a loud and disgusting noise ripped from the general direction of Dad's blanket.

My hand flew to my mouth. "Oh my gosh, was that what I think it was?" I whispered.

Everyone stayed dead silent, and then I heard my dad's voice say, "Um, excuse me."

Bea and I laughed so hard, I'm pretty sure the whole beverage table shook. We tried to be quiet, but she kept snorting. The other couples resumed their conversations, and I nudged Bea to check on the date again.

"Your dad is gone!"

I glanced at my watch. "Right on time. He'll be in the bathroom for a while now. What's she doing?"

"Packing up the rest of the ammunition. She looks . . . disappointed."

"Good. Disappointed is good. Best to shatter expectations right off the bat, don't you think?"

"Well, I sure don't think she's going to be paying hundreds of dollars to go out with the guy again."

Bea pressed closer to the crack. "Wait, your dad is back! He just gave her a handshake. A *handshake*. This has to go down in history as one of the worst dates ever."

"Then my work here is done."

14

That's My Story

I thought I would only beat Dad home by a few minutes, since I walked and he drove, but it was a few hours before he came in the door. I wondered if he'd been helping to clean up after the event, or if he'd just been in the bathroom that whole time.

I turned off the TV as soon as he walked in. I half expected him to come sit next to me, give me a big hug, and tell me he'd been wrong to try this whole dating thing. But he didn't do that.

He dropped the picnic basket on the coffee table and then he stared at me, eyebrows raised.

I shifted and hugged a throw pillow, wishing I could hide underneath it. He didn't exactly look mad, just . . . baffled?

"I packed sandwiches. And chips. And cookies. That was what I packed. I remember putting those items in this basket. Please explain to me why when I sat down to dinner I had . . . other items."

I gulped. I had to think fast, or we could be in big trouble. "Bea and I thought you needed fancier food for your date. Sandwiches are so . . . elementary school. We thought you needed something . . . more special." I looked right at him, right in his eyes, which were the exact same shade of blue as mine. And his face softened. He collapsed on the couch next to me and let out a huge sigh. "Oh. I wondered if that was what happened. I mean, you wouldn't . . ."

He trailed off, and my eyes flicked all around the room, landing everywhere but on his face.

"It's just that . . . I know you aren't loving my going on dates. And for a second I wondered if you had maybe . . ."

I could see Dad struggling for the words. He didn't want to say "packed disgusting things on purpose to ruin my date," because if I had actually been trying to help like I'd led him to believe, then that would be downright rude.

"And what about that bio? Long walks in the cow patties? I definitely do not remember writing that." Dad shook his head.

"Oh, that. I thought it was funny. Did you not think it was funny?" I laughed nervously.

"I guess," he said, shutting his eyes and rubbing his forehead. "You and me . . . we're still a team, right? You want me to be happy and you wouldn't try to . . . embarrass me in my place of employment. Right?" He searched my face, and I tried to make it look as angelic as possible.

"Of course we're still a team." Silently I added, *No thanks to you.*

Dad rubbed at the back of his neck. "You and Bea have clearly never been on a romantic picnic. As a general rule, people try to avoid foods that make you look disgusting when you eat them."

His stomach made a gurgly sound, and he flinched.

I nodded and said, "Ohhh," like I had just learned some new and valuable information. I perked up. "But the passion fruit I packed had to be good, right? Because *passion* is like romantic and stuff."

Dad tilted his head and squinted at the ceiling. "First of all, I had no idea that was what that was. And maybe you didn't notice this, but the seeds look exactly like snot. I gagged when I tried to eat one."

I had noticed. Which is why the passion fruit made it into the basket. "It was still in the fridge from our get-one-of-everything game at the grocery store. I had to Google what it was."

I paused for a second and then asked, "Other than that . . . how was your date with Miss Regina? Are you two going out now?"

I clenched the pillow extra hard and silently repeated, *Say no say no say no*, like a prayer in my head.

Dad snorted. "No. It didn't go very well, to be honest."

I hoped with all my heart that he'd learned his lesson. Dating was too hard. Not only did it have major potential for awkwardness and humiliation, but it also had the power to give you paint-peeling gas. So why did I have a sudden desire to spill the beans and confess everything I'd been up to? The guilt and secrets felt like a wedge between Dad and me.

He shook his head, like he was shaking off the night's terrible events. "It was just a fundraiser. And at least I didn't go on the record as getting the lowest bid. That would have been hard on the old ego."

"I would have bid on you, Dad," I said, leaning my head on his shoulder. "I think you're worth all the money in the world."

I couldn't see his face, but I could feel his smile. "Thanks, Giblet. I feel the same way about you."

I looked down at my hands, wondering if he would say the same thing if he knew all that I had done.

The next night I headed to Bea's for dinner. Usually I just walk right in, but since things were so different in her family lately, I felt like I should probably ring the doorbell. I stood there shivering on the porch, jamming the button about four times. There were noises inside the house. Some clanging, people yelling, some music or the TV on way too loud. Bea wasn't kidding when she said her new life was a circus!

Finally, the door swung open and Bea's mom stood there, looking frazzled but smiling. "Grace!" she said. "How nice to see you!"

She didn't seem like she was expecting me, and I clenched my fingers behind my back. "Um . . . hi, Mrs. Morrison. Bea invited me for dinner," I said.

She smacked herself in the forehead. "Dinner! My goodness! I'd completely forgotten. I wonder if I have anything thawed. . . ." She started to wander toward the kitchen, but she left the door open behind her, so I assumed I was welcome inside.

The living room looked like a bomb had gone off. Books, toys, and teeny-tiny clothes were strewn all over the place. A sock puppet danced on the TV, singing about colors with way too much enthusiasm. There were little orange fishy crackers lined up on the hardwood floor that crunched when I accidentally stepped on them.

Bea came out of the back hallway carrying a squirming, curly-headed boy who looked like he belonged in a toilet paper commercial. The kind of toilet paper that's made of clouds and is soft enough for an angel's booty. Except this kid had a wicked grin on his face.

"Thank goodness you're here," Bea said. "Maybe between the two of us we can keep the little monster out of trouble. Grace, meet Julian. Julian, this is my bestie, Grace."

I took in Bea's sagging shoulders and glassy eyes. She was clearly in distress.

After my mom died, Bea would leave little notes in my mailbox every day with knock-knock jokes or cartoons. And then when Dad started allowing visitors again, she came over every day. Sometimes we didn't even talk; she would just sit beside me or play her guitar. She was there for me when my whole world had fallen apart. So now it was my turn to be there for her. I reached over and took the sticky toddler out of her arms.

Bea brought a shaky hand to her forehead. "Just today he's eaten BoBo's dog food, smeared pudding on the wall, and set the world's record for most times out of bed during a nap."

"Um . . . where's your dad?" I asked, bouncing Julian on my hip.

"Diaper run. You know they go through like five of those things a day? Personally, I think Dad just volunteers so he can get away from all the noise."

Bea's mom yelled something from the kitchen, but it

sounded like her head was in a cabinet, so we went in there to see what she wanted.

"Does Grace like tuna casserole?" Mrs. Morrison called from the pantry.

"Yes! Anything is fine!" I said, even though to be real honest, tuna casserole tastes like fishy snot.

Julian started crying at that moment, so maybe he wasn't excited about tuna casserole either. Bea scrunched her face up at him, reaching over to tickle him under his chin. "What's wrong now?"

He wiped a tiny fist across his already slippery nose and then grabbed a handful of Bea's hair and yanked. She howled. They glared at each other. So this was what it looked like to have your family rearranged. No thank you.

"Mom!" Bea called, rubbing at her scalp with her free hand. "Can you take him for a while so I can hang out with Grace?"

Mrs. Morrison emerged from the pantry with her arms full of ingredients. "Can you two watch him while I throw some dinner together? He's hungry—that's why he's mad. Give him a snack and we'll eat in thirty."

Bea muttered something under her breath about how she'd been watching him all day, and I followed her back into the living room. She found a crumpled bag of fishy crackers, gave me a handful, ate a few herself, and dumped the rest on the coffee table, next to where I sat Julian down on the floor. He grabbed a fistful and instantly got two hundred percent happier.

"Did you see that? How Mom just pawned him off on us? That's pretty much the story of my life now." Bea scowled and ate a cracker.

I watched Julian paw at the crackers with chubby fingers. "Is it even a little bit fun? I always thought having a baby in the house would be like having a personal living doll. Can you dress him up at least?"

Bea shrugged. "Not really. He hates getting his clothes changed. It's not worth the screaming."

This whole thing was so unfair that I felt outraged on Bea's behalf.

Bea leaned closer and spoke in a conspiratorial whisper. "My parents missed my gymnastics meet last night. They've never missed one before. I had to get a ride with Becca because they said they were just too busy and exhausted to go."

"It was just one meet," I said, trying desperately to find a silver lining here. "I'm sure once things settle down they'll be able to find time for both of you."

"*And* it was Mom's turn to bring snacks. Which I reminded her of two days in a row. Guess who had to explain to everyone why they were going to be starving on the way home?"

That was harsh. Snacks were my favorite part of sports games.

Bea closed her eyes and leaned back on the couch. "I think I could sleep for a week."

I lowered my voice enough that I hoped Mrs. Morrison wouldn't be able to hear me from the kitchen. "This isn't fair at all! I mean, you didn't sign up for this. And now this kid that your parents have adopted is just like . . . ruining your life!"

I thought Bea might've had something to say about that, but she'd fallen asleep. I covered her with the blanket that's always draped over the couch and waited for my tuna casserole. Julian stared at me with big round eyes and continuously stuffed his face with crackers. He was just giggling, drooling proof that one little addition had the potential to wreck a whole entire family.

15

A Lid for Every Pot

When I got home after choking down my portion of tuna-cheese slime, I found Dad camped out on the couch with his laptop. *Jungle Survivor* was on the TV, but he was so focused on the computer that he didn't even look up when I walked in. In fact, I think I could have thrown a flaming bag of dog poo at his head and he wouldn't have noticed. Something was up.

"Hey, Dad," I said, sitting down next to him on the couch and waving my hand in front of his face to try to bring him out of his stupor.

"Hey," he said, and then, "Do you think I'm more of a Kennedy or a Clinton?"

"Huh?"

Dad's face turned the color of pistachio pudding as he realized who he was talking to. "Oh, it's nothing. It's for my profile on this website." He tried to subtly turn his screen away from me.

A whooshing sound filled my ears, and panic sent my hands shaking. What was this fresh madness? Dad was on a dating site now?

"You're more of a John Quincy Adams, I'd say." I tried to keep my voice casual, but Dad's eyebrows shot up in surprise.

"Old JQA, huh? Maybe if I grew in my chops . . ." Dad started stroking at his sideburns. "Wait . . . wasn't he the one who was always swimming naked in the river?"

I shrugged. "He was in tune with nature."

Dad started typing away furiously, and I risked a lean in his direction to get a glimpse of the screen. The website was called A Lid for Every Pot, and it seemed to be a dating site for people with geeky hobbies. Dad was fully entrenched in the history-buff section, filling out his profile information. He'd already uploaded a picture of himself wearing his stovepipe hat, like Abraham Lincoln.

I sat there watching *Jungle Survivor* and listening to Dad introducing himself to future wives. I wondered if he even mentioned me in his profile.

A man on *Jungle Survivor* ditched the rest of his team to claim the prize in the challenge. He jumped up and down with excitement about the five-course dinner and the night at a luxury hotel that he'd be enjoying alone. His teammates glared at him. I understood their rage at his betrayal. But unlike those jungle survivors, I wasn't going to let Dad leave me high and dry in the pulsing tropical sun.

"Hey, so next weekend we should finish the baseboards in the attic," I said, watching his face closely. If he had any dates planned, he would definitely flinch or something.

"Well . . . maybe. We'll have to wait and see." He glanced at his laptop screen one more time before shutting the lid.

"Oh really. Not sure what you might have going on, huh?"

"I just like to keep my plans free and breezy, you know? I'm a fly-by-the-seat-of-my-pants kind of guy."

Since when? We couldn't even plan weekends now? I couldn't count on my dad being around or finishing projects that we'd started together because he *might* get a date?

He finally glanced at me long enough to see the pout forming on my face. "Hey there, Giblet. We'll get your room done. I just can't say for sure exactly when."

I crossed my arms and harrumphed and told Dad I was going to bed. He kissed my forehead and booped my nose (which I hate) and told me he'd be up in a few minutes to say my prayers with me. He never came.

With Potus in a ball at my feet, I lay there listening to the sounds of the house. Dad turned off the TV around ten and headed to bed. I stared at the ceiling, thinking about my new room and all the time that me and Dad could have been working on it if he hadn't been brainwashed to find true love in a hurry.

Finally, Dad's snoring reached Civil War cannon levels of loud, so I snuck downstairs in my sock feet. His computer was still sitting on the couch where he'd left it. For a second I rested my hands on the keys and wondered if what I was about to do was right. I'd never betrayed my dad's trust this way before. I mean, if you can forget the fart basket and the stuffed-chicken sabotage. But hacking into his computer? That was taking things to the next level.

Potus, who had followed me downstairs, gave me a judgy look. "What?" I whispered. "Dad didn't even come to say my prayers with me like he said he would." The dog tilted his head as if to say, *Is that all?*

"No, that is not all. He also couldn't squeeze out any time for me in his busy date-filled weekend."

The dog just kept staring. It's like he knew I was doing something I wasn't supposed to. Or maybe *I* knew I was doing something I wasn't supposed to. Animals are very sensitive to human feelings. Including guilt. "Look, dog, I know what I'm doing."

Potus sighed and put his head down on his paws, as if he was tired of arguing with me.

I let out a long breath and touched the pad to wake up the screen. And there was the dating website, right where Dad had left off.

His username and password were saved on Lidforeverypot.com, so all I had to do was click Sign In. That's how much my dad did NOT worry that I would mess with his stuff. *Gulp*. And there at the top of the page was his goofy, smiling face. Staring at me with that silly stovepipe hat on his head that we'd gotten at the Lincoln Library last summer. My stomach churned.

Maybe Pastor Davy was too geeky even for these geek chicks? I mean, his profile said he loved presidential trivia, history, and *Jungle Survivor*. I did smile for a fraction of a second when I noticed he'd called me the love of his life and his pride and joy. At least he wasn't hiding his single-dad status.

A tiny red notification dot with the number ten in it signaled from his mailbox. I clicked it, my fingers shaking. Ten matches in the first couple of hours! Ten women who were charmed by him wearing a hat that looked like a canister of oatmeal. *How is this happening?*

I started answering emails as fast as my fingers would go.

Sorry but I'm deathly allergic to dogs. (Nope.)

Sorry but I actually hate all movies about Nixon. (Lies.)

Sorry but I might be moving to Guam. (Ha ha.)

Sorry but I'm not sure my daughter would approve. (My favorite.)

Now that the inbox was clear, I put my real plan into action. It took me approximately ten minutes to set up a different Lid for Every Pot account, steal a profile picture off Google, and write up a bio that would make Dad drool.

"Clarissa Washington" lived in the next town over. She was a historian and a museum curator. She liked to dress up like Jackie Kennedy. She played the accordion (I figured she had to have at least *one* flaw, or Dad would think she was too good to be true).

Clarissa sent Dad a simple note saying she was interested in what she'd read of his profile, and would he want to meet up the following Saturday for lunch? Noon at Ziggy's in Springdale.

I thought about all the weekend road trips and Saturdays full of projects and silly pajama days with my dad and how all that time would definitely go to someone else if he started dating seriously. I took one last shaky breath before clicking Send.

Dad would be at Ziggy's for lunch on Saturday, but Clarissa Washington would not make an appearance. Dad was about to learn an important lesson about people on the internet not always being who they say they are, a lesson he'd pounded into my head since elementary school. Some pots don't need lids. Some pots do a great job cooking stuff all by themselves.

16

Lasagna Lessons

Dad left for his date at eleven-thirty without telling me his plans. He had a bounce in his step and gel in his hair. I felt my heart squeeze as his truck pulled out of the drive-way. Poor sucker. Dad would show up at Ziggy's exactly on time. He'd request a table for two with a twinkle in his eye. And then he was going to wait, and wait, and wait.

I came home from watching movies at Bea's house to what sounded like a plane being dismantled. I stepped over the cookbooks littering the living room floor and discovered the crashing was actually my dad throwing pots and pans around in the kitchen.

"Hey, Dad." I dodged a large puddle of water in the middle of the checked tile floor. "What kind of science experiment is this?"

Dad's cheeks were red, either from exertion or from

heat. Every burner flamed on the gas stove, even though there were only two pans on there. It was sweaty hot.

"I was in the mood for lasagna." He had three different dish towels flung over his shoulders, like he'd thrown them up there and then promptly forgotten where they were.

"Lasagna?"

He didn't stop rummaging in the cabinet. "Yeah. Just like Mom used to make, remember?"

I did remember. My mom made the most amazing lasagna. It had so much cheese on top she had to smash it down with her hands so it wouldn't fall out of the pan. I used to request lasagna for my birthday dinner every year, and Mom made a big deal out of fixing it for me. She would stick the birthday candles in the cheesy top and let me make a bonus lasagna wish in addition to my cake wish.

Dad yanked a jar of marinara out of the cabinet and immediately dropped it on the floor, shards of glass exploding and covering the walls and cabinets with chunky red sauce.

"Cheese and rice," Dad muttered. He wasn't using real swear words yet, so I figured it wasn't too late to fix this situation.

"It's okay. Hey, let's call Ziggy's and order a lasagna to go! We could go pick it up and then come back here and—"

"No Ziggy's," Dad said fervently. "I'm making it. . . . I

have Mom's recipe right here." He used one of the towels from his shoulder to wipe sauce off a thick cookbook.

I surveyed the disaster and the sad look on Dad's face and turned off the burners that weren't heating any pots. This catastrophe was at least partially my fault. Well, mine and Clarissa Washington's. I grabbed a dish towel and crouched down to help mop up the sauce-and-glass mess.

"You okay, Dad?"

"This never happened when she made it," Dad muttered, attempting to scoop the goop into a dustpan.

"Do you have another jar of sauce?" I asked, plucking a large chunk of glass out of the sludge.

Dad stood up and scanned the contents of the cabinet. "We have salsa. . . . Do you think that would work?"

"Um . . ."

He unscrewed the jar and added the contents to the crunchy-looking meat scorched to the bottom of a frying pan. I tried not to think about how that would taste.

"Here, I'll drain the noodles." I grabbed the pot off the burner and quickly dropped it, screaming in pain.

"Grace! You gotta use one of those fluffy mittens when you touch hot pans!"

"Oh yeah. I forgot." I ran my angry red palms under cool water to try to take some of the sting out.

"Here, let me do it." Dad pulled some long white socks onto his hands, up to his elbows, and I burst out laughing.

"I thought you said you had to wear fluffy mittens!"

Dad straightened his back and stuck out his chin. "Well, we don't have any of those. At least not any I could find . . ."

I reached into the drawer where the oven mitts lived and gave him two.

"Huh. What do you know?"

"I know how to take frozen pizza out of the oven," I said.

"Well, let me drain at least." He awkwardly tried to tilt the heavy pot to dump the water out while keeping the noodles in with a wooden spoon.

"Here." I handed him a colander from a top cabinet, and he gave me a quizzical look. "I also know how to drain the noodles for my mac and cheese."

The noodles dropped into the colander in one large stuck-together blob. Dad and I both stared at the ball of gluey ribbons.

"Is that what it's supposed to look like?" he asked.

"How should I know?" I said, but I had a sneaking suspicion that the answer was no.

Dad got out a large glass casserole dish and began layering the shreds of noodles he could loosen from the ball with the meat and salsa mixture. Then a layer of cottage cheese (we didn't have any ricotta, like the recipe called for). He finished the concoction by smashing an entire bag of mozzarella on the top, just like Mom used to do. As he pressed the mess in the pan, a single tear ran down his face.

I stared in horror. Dad didn't cry! I mean, I hadn't seen him cry since those first dark weeks without Mom. He was the strong one! I guess part of me thought he never missed her the way I did. But that tear told a different story. Guilt about all the ruined dates I'd orchestrated filled my guts. I put my hand on his arm, and he wiped angrily at the traitorous tear. "Must be the onions," he said gruffly. But there weren't any onions in there, and we both knew it.

While the lasagna (or whatever you would call the mess we'd made) smoldered, the smoke detector went off, and I had to help Dad wave dish towels at the black clouds billowing out of the oven.

"I don't know what happened! It's not even supposed to be done yet!" Dad yelled over the alarm.

I squinted through the smoke to the bottom of the oven, where the extra cheese had slipped off the top of the lasagna and made a blackened, broiling mess.

I slammed the oven door shut and turned it off, waving my dish towel toward the alarm until the screeching stopped.

Dad's face drooped. "Maybe we should microwave it the rest of the way?"

"Yeah, sure," I said, but there was no way I was eating

that mess. I dumped the disgusting lump in the microwave and then herded Dad into the living room and plopped him in front of the TV.

I crossed my arms. "This is all Miss Donna and Miss Marge's fault," I said, staring at whatever was happening on whatever show we both were not watching.

"What are you talking about?" Dad's voice sounded tired.

"Those busybodies from church! They got it into your head that you should go on dates and stuff. They're the ones making you sad."

Dad sighed and rubbed his hands down his face. "This has very little to do with the church or those ladies, Grace. I know it must seem like that to you, but the truth of the matter is, I *want* to start dating again. I'm lonely."

My stomach turned to ice. This whole time I'd been thinking those ladies were putting thoughts in Dad's head, trying to get all up in his business. But it was *his* choice. *He* wanted to date. He said he was lonely, and I believed him this time. His face was twisted miserably as he stared at the TV, and I couldn't stop thinking about that single tear running down his face.

I felt something inside me break. A wall that had been resisting finally crumbled. I couldn't stand to see my dad unhappy. Confused, sure. Gassy, you betcha. But I wasn't going to cause him to be unhappy anymore. If going on dates was what he needed, I wasn't going to interfere. My meddling days were over.

I cleared my throat. "You won't be lonely for long, Dad. Somewhere out there is a lady just dying for some terrible puns and history trivia." My voice softened to a whisper. "Don't give up, okay? You should be happy."

Dad smiled and squeezed my knee. "Hey, who said anything about giving up? This is your old man we're talking about."

"I think we should give up on that lasagna. What do you say we order some Chinese food?"

The microwave beep was accented by a terrible smell.

I hopped up to grab the menu, and Dad followed me into the kitchen. We stood in the doorway, surveying the clouds of smoke, the puddles of water and sauce, the chunk of unused noodles still in the sink.

Dad glanced at Mom's open cookbook on the counter. It looked wilted and a bit singed around the edges. He let out a sigh. "Fine. Chinese it is."

I pulled out paper plates and napkins. (Hey, I wasn't going to do any extra dishes after the mountain we already had in the sink!) And when the delivery guy came I thanked him profusely and gave him an extra-big tip. I managed to make Dad laugh by balancing my chopstick under my nose like a mustache and somehow the sadness lifted by a fraction and we were able to exhale.

My dad was sad. And maybe lonely? And missing something in his life, I guess. And as much as I wished it wasn't true, I needed to start thinking about him more than me and stop undermining his dates. If going on boring old non-sabotaged dates was what my dad needed, I wasn't going to stand in his way.

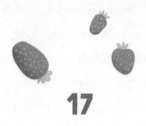

17

Waving the White Flag

The next Saturday, I threw on a sequined mermaid sweat-shirt and fish-scale-printed leggings and met up with Bea at Springdale's only coffee shop. We were supposed to be working on our famous-American reports, but I couldn't imagine cracking open a book when my head was so full of my dad and me and lasagna.

A quiet buzz of voices mixed with the clanking of dishes and the whirl of the coffee bean grinder. The smell of fresh-baked muffins wafted through the air.

Bea gave me a quick hug when she saw me, and we both ordered frappes with double whip and dragged our stuffed-full backpacks to a quiet table in the back.

After a few seconds of getting all her books and papers and notecards stacked and in order, Bea pulled a bag of Skittles out of her backpack and started divvying them up. Her blond hair was combed and decorated with a pink headband that coordinated with her pants. She was clean and neat and organized. Basically the opposite of my kitchen last weekend.

"Have you ever seen one of your parents have a complete and total meltdown?" I asked as I pulled my books out of my pack.

She scrunched up her nose. "Until recently I would have said no, but the other night my mom put one of Julian's diapers on her head and pretended to bop herself over and over again with his stuffed bear."

"Uh . . . why?" I asked, eyebrows raised.

"Julian thought it was funny. And he has this hilarious little laugh. Mom would do pretty much anything to get him to do it."

"Oh, well . . . I was talking about like crying and stuff," I said, not meeting Bea's eyes.

"Hmm . . . I've seen my mom cry a few times, but not really my dad. Why? What's going on?" She scooted the pile of red and green Skittles toward me and took a long sip of her coffee.

I filled her in on Chef Dad's tearful dinner menu and her mouth dropped open.

"Oh Mylanta. Do you think it was because you've been messing with all his dates and now he thinks he's hopelessly unlovable?"

My guts twisted as I remembered the miserable look on

Dad's face. "I hope not. That's totally not what I meant to happen. The last person on earth who should feel unlovable is my dad. He's the best. And I feel terrible about all the trouble we've caused him."

"*We've* caused him? Speak for yourself. One hundred percent of these ideas have been yours, and I merely went along for the ride," Bea said flatly.

I smiled. "That's why you're my best friend. I promise I won't implicate you in any future interrogations." I watched a guy carry his tray of drinks over to his table. A pretty lady grabbed her coffee off the tray and then set the other two smaller cups in front of their two kids. They all smiled at each other and I had to look away.

My mom used to love this place and she would take Dad and me here a lot on Saturday mornings. Dad would practice his preaching and I would order a pastry and Mom would sip her coffee. She was great at giving Dad ideas for funnier sermon illustrations. They would laugh together as he scribbled notes in the margins. I realized I hadn't given Dad any sermon ideas in a long, long time.

"My dad is lonely. And not just missing-Mom kind of lonely, but, like, big-fat-hole-in-his-heart kind of lonely. You know?"

Saying the words out loud made them more real. I clutched at my frappe cup, even though my fingers felt frozen.

Bea nodded. "So, I guess that's it? Quit derailing his dates if it's making him cry over his pasta."

I cringed. "Yeah, I guess so."

Bea cleared her throat, and her eyes traveled all around the room. "I'm not saying I think you're wrong . . . ," she started. Which instantly made me think she totally thought I was wrong.

My eyes bulged at her over my frappe. "What?"

She pulled her straw out and licked the whipped cream off. "It's just . . . what if letting your dad be happy . . . makes you super unhappy?"

I had a sudden vision of Dad ditching me to go play shuffleboard with Miss Regina. Missing my birthday to shop for cantaloupes with Rachel. Spending all our road trip money on presents for White Pants.

I took a deep breath. And then ate some Skittles. And then washed them down with some coffee. Finally, I lifted my eyes to Bea's. "I guess if that's what it takes, if that's what he needs, then it's just something I'll have to deal with."

The combination of sugar and caffeine was kicking in, and I stuffed my hands under my legs to keep them from vibrating. Or maybe it was the fact that my life was falling apart that made me shaky.

"Whew," Bea said, and then, when she saw my hurt face, quickly added, "I'm just relieved we aren't going to be doing any more scheming. I wasn't meant for a life of crime!"

The iceberg of guilt in my chest melted just a tiny fraction after we'd officially decided to keep our noses out of Dad's business. Maybe now I could just work on fixing things between the members of Team Gravy. No more lies. No more pranks. No more plans. "Yeah," I said. "Maybe I wasn't either."

18

This Is a Test

Sunday afternoon meant more construction time with Dad after church. Putting the trim up in the attic was taking a lot longer than I had thought it would, but I wasn't even mad about it because at least that meant more time for Team Gravy.

"Here, hold this piece in place while I nail," Dad said, whipping a hammer out of his tool belt. The funny thing was, he never remembered to put any of the tools back in the tool belt and was constantly losing them.

"Got it," I said, holding the trim snugly against the wall. The corners matched up perfectly, thanks to my awesome work with the angle saw.

"Just a few more pieces to go and we can call this a wrap," Dad said, wiping his brow with his flannel shirt.

"Still needs paint and carpet," I reminded him. Then

it would really feel like a finished space. I couldn't wait to move all my stuff up here.

The rest of the trim pieces went up with only one minor problem—luckily, we'd measured too long instead of too short, so it was easily fixed. When the last board was nailed to the wall, Dad declared it was break time. He sat down on the rough wooden subfloor, and I jumped up to get cold cans of soda out of the mini-fridge. The tiny refrigerator was literally my only possession that had found its way up here so far, but it came in handy during construction.

"Cheers! To the best new room a girl could ask for!" I said, sitting on the floor next to Dad, and he clunked his Coke can into mine.

Dad took a long swig.

Even though it was early March, which most places would consider spring, in Missouri it was still cold and gray. There were some dirty patches of snow still piled up in parking lots and everyone was just ready for winter to be over. The magic of the snow is definitely dead by March. My eyes watched some random snowflakes that drifted by the window and I hoped they didn't plan on staying long. "Hey, you know what I thought about this morning?"

"What?"

"That night of the blizzard. When I was ten. Do you remember?" I asked.

Dad smiled. "Yes. How could I forget? I think I got frostbite."

I laughed, remembering the night so many years ago like it was yesterday. I'd gone to bed on a regular weeknight, but in the middle of the night, I awoke to Dad shaking my shoulder. "Come with me," he said. "You gotta see this." He bundled my sleepy self up in my warmest coat, mittens, and hat. And then we walked hand in hand into what looked like the inside of a snow globe. It felt like magic. I hadn't been bothered by the biting wind or the bitter cold. I'd just stared as the snowflakes danced in the streetlights and the neighborhood transformed into something out of a Christmas storybook. Dad and I watched the snow until we were both shivering and our ears hurt from the wind and cold. But I remembered the feeling of being the only two people in the world. Just me and Dad. And thinking that it felt perfect.

"What made you think of that?" Dad asked, but I just shrugged. I didn't want to tell him I was still wishing we were the only two people in the world. Not after I'd just vowed to support his new dating goals. But as I watched his face, I could still remember the snowflakes that landed on his eyelashes that night.

"A special memory, I guess. Just the two of us." I smiled at Dad, and he suddenly looked like his T-shirt collar was too tight.

"I'm gonna order a pizza tonight. What kind do you want?"

"We always get Hawaiian," I said, cautiously studying his change in body language.

"Right. Right. I'll get one Hawaiian, and maybe one pepperoni. Everyone likes pepperoni, right?"

"I guess. Why two pizzas? That's a lot for just us two."

Dad paused and flicked at an invisible speck on his knee. "I invited someone over for dinner. An old friend from high school. Her name is Gretchen."

There was a long pause. I didn't know what Dad wanted me to say about this. He'd invited a woman over to our house for dinner. Was she his old girlfriend?

"Gretchen," I repeated, like some kind of not very intelligent robot. I glanced over at Dad's face. He blushed. Or maybe he was just sweaty from construction. The corners of his mouth were curled up in a smile, though. And when he looked at me, it was almost like he was asking my permission.

It took all of my brainpower to remember that this was what I wanted. I wanted my dad to be happy. But a tiny part of me felt like this was some kind of test. A date at home would be so very easy to sabotage. . . .

"So, you know her from high school," I said cautiously. I needed more information.

"Yeah," Dad said. "We were actually friends when we

were little kids. I used to cut the hair off her Barbie dolls, and she used to put frogs in my backpack."

Frogs in your backpack, huh. Maybe Gretchen and I had more in common than I would like to admit. I squashed the urge to put salt in her iced tea and thumbtacks on her chair. At least for now.

"I'm sure she'll just *croak* for some pepperoni, then," I said, giving my dad the wide-open *Get it?* look he always gives me.

"Well played, Giblet. Well played."

Dad jumped in the shower to wash all the attic stink off him, and I decided I'd better try my best to make a good impression too.

I flicked through my closet and settled on a lime-green sweater with a cute lemon pattern. My grandma Bette had sent it from New York last month, and I hoped it might cheer me up. I paired it with a purple sequined skirt. As I pulled the sweater over my head, I worried that I wouldn't be able to control my urge to get rid of Gretchen. I just kept telling myself I only wanted Dad to be happy.

I pulled my hair into two pigtails and then wound them into buns, Princess Leia–style. After selecting a Dr Pepper

Lip Smacker, I gave myself my most winning smile in the mirror.

Gretchen would love me. And she'd love my dad. And they'd love each other. And even if nobody loved anyone, everyone loved pizza, so it would all be okay.

At exactly six o'clock there was a knock on the door. I flung it open and stared at the lady standing on our porch. She was a lot prettier than I was expecting. She wore a long gray coat, with a soft flowery top underneath. Her jewelry sparkled, and red curls framed her face. Everything about her looked expensive, and her fancy perfume punched me in the nose. She smiled at me, and I smiled back.

"Hello, Gretchen. Nice to meet you. I'm Grace, and I believe you used to bully my dad when you were kids."

She smiled and cocked one eyebrow. "Hello, Grace. I'll tell you some stories about your dad, and then you can decide who the bully was." Somehow that one cocked eyebrow made it feel like me and Gretchen were in on a joke or something. I instantly liked her just a little bit.

"Is that the pizza guy?" Dad leapt down the stairs, still buttoning his blue shirt. He saw Gretchen and froze on the last stair, a big, goofy grin on his face.

"Hi, Davy!" She leaned over the threshold.

I held the door open even more. "Won't you come in?"

She stepped inside, and Dad bounded across the room

in three large steps and shook her hand like she was a car salesman or something.

"Grace, I see you've met Gretchen. Fun story, Gretchen and I recently ran into each other at the DMV. I was re-taking my eye exam, and I thought it would be funny to loudly spell . . . well, I don't need to tell you exactly what I spelled. The point is, the examiner did not laugh, but Gretchen cracked up, and when I turned around to see who got me . . ." He looked at her and they grinned at each other.

"It was pretty funny to hear a preacher spell *POOP* at the top of his lungs," Gretchen said.

Dad took Gretchen's coat and hung it on the rack. "I couldn't believe it. There she was. The girl who used to steal all my paper route money."

Gretchen had the good sense to look slightly embarrassed about that one. "Well," she said, "candy you buy with stolen money tastes better."

Gretchen walked around our living room, touching and commenting on things, while Dad followed her. She seemed nice, although not too interested in me. Dad, on the other hand, was acting like a kid who'd eaten too much sugary cereal for breakfast—all sweaty and jittery and talking a mile a minute.

His face relaxed when the doorbell rang again. "Ah, the food's here." While he paid the pizza guy, Gretchen and I sat silently at the kitchen table. I smiled at her. She smiled at me. Then she examined her manicure.

I was grateful when Dad returned and we could dig into the piping-hot pizza.

"So, Gretchen, what have you been doing for the last . . . twenty years?" Dad asked, smiling. He struggled with the packet of hot peppers, and instead of just opening, the envelope exploded in a confetti of red flakes all over the table.

"Smooth move," I whispered. Geez, maybe I didn't even have to pull any pranks to ruin Dad's dates. His nerves seem to be doing a pretty good job of that without any help from me.

"Well, I work as an auditor," she said.

There was a weird pause where I hoped my dad would jump in and say something charming, but no such luck, so I kept things rolling. "And what is an auditor again?"

Gretchen smiled with her extra-white teeth. "An auditor checks to make sure that individuals and businesses are complying with tax laws."

"That's so funny, because I've always said a pastor is like an auditor *of souls*." I crossed my arms and smiled.

Dad smirked at me. "Is that what you've always said? You literally just asked what an auditor is." We all chuckled at that, but then silence settled around us like deep snow. Turns out being an auditor is not a rich well of conversational topics.

We took cheesy bites of pizza and stared at our laps.

"So, what do you think about my dad? He's great, right? Quite a catch, if you ask me."

Dad kicked me under the table. It hurt my heart more than it hurt my shin. But Gretchen just laughed. "He is pretty cool."

I snorted at that. Because my dad is a lot of things, but *cool* is definitely not one of them.

Gretchen told us all about her job (I zoned out), her car (just bought it), and her lake house (how much did auditors get paid?). Dad seemed to be losing interest even faster than I was. Finally, she started talking about her tiny Pomeranian puppy, a topic I could get behind!

"Oh, my mom always wanted one of those dogs! They are so cute and fluffy and . . ."

The grown-ups looked very uncomfortable all of a sudden, and I didn't think about what I'd said until everyone went silent. We all just shoveled pizza in our mouths, thinking about the big dumb elephant in the room, which I'd just named.

My mom.

Who was dead.

Was I not allowed to talk about my mom in front of Dad's dates? Was that a rule or something? It felt like a pokey wooden sliver under my heart.

Wow, dating is harder than it looks on TV.

135

It was so quiet, we all jumped out of our seats when there was another knock on the door.

"Who in the heck would that be?" I said.

"I'll get it," Dad said, springing to his feet.

"Hey, Team Gravy!" Miss O'Connor burst through the door and froze when she saw us gathered around the table. "Oh, sorry. Didn't know you had company."

"No, no, it's okay." Dad grabbed the stuff out of Miss O'Connor's hands. "Lemme help you with those bags. Uh, Gretchen, this is Olivia O'Connor. She's our friend and Grace's history teacher."

They nodded at each other, and Miss O'Connor bustled inside. She had a way of filling up a room, like she had this energy pulsing out of her. It was a happy energy, and I liked it.

Dad peeked in the bag. "What's in here?"

Miss O'Connor grinned. "Well, Grace was telling me all about the costumes she's making for the World's Fair, and I told her I'd look for fabric the next time I went to Branson."

"What costumes?" Dad asked, glancing at me as I grinned from ear to ear.

"Surprise! We were hired to be reenactors at the St. Louis World's Fare Heritage Festival this summer! Remember, I told you about it? You and I will be cosplaying the most popular president and first daughter duo in history—

Teddy and Alice Roosevelt, who famously visited the World's Fair in 1904."

"You're going to dress up in costumes?" Gretchen asked, letting out this high-pitched laugh that sounded like a hyena.

Dad said, "I'm one hundred percent on board with this." His cheeks pinked up, but he gave me an extra-tight hug. "Why not? We were already planning on road-tripping to St. Louis this summer. Got to rub that billiken belly."

"Yeah!" I said. "And . . . I had another great idea. While we're there and all dressed up, let's re-create the photo of Four-Times-Great-Granny Juliet."

Gretchen smiled tightly. "Miss O'Connor should give you extra credit in history class after all that work."

Miss O'Connor laughed, and I shook my head. "That's one class where I really don't need the extra credit."

Dad held up the tan linen fabric that would presumably become his suit. "This is perfect, Olivia, thanks so much."

She blushed, and it made the tiny freckles on her nose stand out even more. "Oh, and I finished reading *The Life and Times of Woodrow Wilson*. It's fascinating. You want to borrow it?"

Dad grinned. "You know I do! Hey, you want some pizza?"

Miss O'Connor gave Gretchen one more glance before

looking at her wrist (which didn't have a watch) and claiming she was late for something.

As soon as she was gone it was like all the sunshine had been sucked out of the room. Dad almost seemed to deflate. I looked from him to Gretchen, then from him to the door my teacher had just exited through, and it was like a bolt of lightning hit me in the brains. Gretchen wasn't the one making Dad's whole face light up like a birthday cake. Miss O'Connor was.

19

Measure Twice, Cut Once

"You cut it too small." I squinted at Dad's costume fabric spread out on the floor.

"That's madness. I measured once, cut twice."

I smacked myself in the forehead. "It's measure twice, cut once!"

I was close to wadding the whole mess up and throwing it at him, when he started to chuckle. "I kid, I kid. . . ."

"Dad, we don't have time for your shenanigans. Do you think it's easy to just whip up an accurate turn-of-the-century ensemble?"

Dad riffled through the directions we'd printed off the internet. "This is a lot of work just to sweat through a festival while people try to take selfies with you."

I stood up and stretched my tired back. *Who knew sewing was so flippin' hard?* "Maybe we need to call for backup."

"Come on now, this is a Team Gravy project and we need to see it through until the end."

I'd had a brilliant idea this morning. After seeing the spark between my dad and Miss O'Connor last weekend, I wanted to see if my instincts were right. "I'm not saying we quit. I'm saying we might need to get someone to help us who actually knows what she's doing."

Dad rubbed the stubble on his chin and turned the directions another hundred and eighty degrees. "I see the logic there. Should I call Grandma?"

I groaned. "Grandma is all the way in New York. How's she going to help us?"

He shrugged. "I dunno. Maybe she can explain to me what a 'seam allowance' is. Are we paying these guys allowance now?"

"Ha ha. Call Miss O'Connor." I studied his face for any kind of reaction, but he just chuckled at his own joke as he dialed Miss O'Connor, and in fact he thought it was so hilarious he repeated it to her. He yukked it up for a few more minutes, and after he'd wiped the tears from his eyes, he explained our situation. There was some Charlie Brown's teacher–style mumbling on the other end, and then he said, "Okay, great. We'll see you soon."

He hung up the phone still shaking his head at the genius of his own dumb pun.

Miss O'Connor arrived in twenty minutes, hauling a sewing machine under one arm and swinging a wicker basket on the other. "Here I come to save the day!" she sang, to the tune of the *Jungle Survivor* theme song.

"Seamstress Olivia's on her way!" my dad continued the song.

"Ain't nobody gonna stand in my way!" they sang together, but then they went quiet because neither one of them could think of a rhyming last line. When they read the puzzled expressions on each other's faces, they both burst out laughing.

Bingo. Sparks.

"You guys are total nerds," I said, digging through the basket for a pair of scissors capable of cutting fabric.

"Takes one to know one," Dad said, sticking his tongue out.

"So what are we doing here, kids?" Miss O'Connor asked, flopping on the floor next to me. "I see you've already mangled your fabric."

"It's harder than it looks," Dad said, rubbing the back of his neck and grinning sheepishly.

"Summer will be here before you know it, and Dad and I have an adoring audience of history enthusiasts to entertain!" I lifted my chin and grinned.

Miss O'Connor smiled. "I can't think of a more perfect

pair to portray Teddy and Alice. I'd like to get my picture taken with the two of you myself." She cracked her knuckles. "Lemme see what I can do."

I headed to the kitchen for a soda, but Miss O'Connor called me out. "Where do you think you're going?"

"Kitchen? Drink? So thirsty . . ." I mimed choking from thirst.

"Hey, Alice Roosevelt, your ruffly dress isn't going to sew itself. Get over here and learn something."

"Ha ha!" Dad pointed and laughed until Miss O'Connor swatted at his finger. "Don't laugh. You have to watch too. There's a test on this later."

That knocked the smile off Dad's face.

"Okay, the first problem I see here is that you forgot to fold the fabric before you started cutting. The good news is, I think I can match this edge up with that, and lay the pieces like this—"

"But that's not what it looks like on the pattern!" Dad interrupted.

"Well, we are improvising. Do you want a front *and a back* to your pants?"

Dad scratched his head. "Do I get to pick which one?"

I made a sick face. "Ew, Dad, gross!"

"What? You don't think Teddy Roosevelt ever delivered a speech with his backside flapping in the breeze?"

Miss O'Connor chuckled and shook her head. "So what,

pray tell, have you two been up to since last Sunday?" She put little pins with colorful balls on the end all the way around the pattern pieces and then handed me her scissors. "Cut, please."

"Trying to figure out which location on our presidential bucket list we want to hit up next. See the map on the wall?"

Hung over the old piano was a pastel-colored map glued to a corkboard. A few lonely pins were stuck in "wacky historical sites" Dad and I had already visited.

"On Sundays when Dad isn't preaching, we try to make it to the closer ones. In three weeks we're going to Independence, Missouri, to visit the Truman Library!"

She grimaced.

"What's wrong with Harry S. Truman?"

"Oh, nothing. How come you aren't preaching that Sunday, Pastor Davy?" She batted her eyelashes at him.

"It's Youth Sunday. The high school kids will have just gotten back from a retreat, and Pastor Steve is talking about everything they learned."

Miss O'Connor flinched. "I suspected as much."

Dad crossed his arms and glared at her. "You have a problem with Youth Sunday?"

"No, I have a problem with Pastor Steve. He spits when he talks, and he uses too many sports analogies."

I giggled. "And he wears his hair all spiky so people will

think he's young and cool, like we can't see that he's going bald."

She laughed. "Well, there's always that to look forward to. Maybe I'll attend Bedside Baptist that Sunday. I might be getting sick." She fake coughed and tried to look pathetic.

Dad tapped his fist on his lips, which transformed into a lopsided smile. "So you enjoy my preaching, huh? Not too heavy for ya? Spiritually enlightening with a dash of entertainment?"

Dad was seriously flirting. With my teacher. But I was strangely okay with it. I liked to see him having fun and goofing off, not being all stiff and formal like at the pizza dinner with Gretchen.

Miss O'Connor handed him the front and back of his pants, which she had skillfully pinned together. "Well, you're no Pastor Steve. . . ."

Dad looked momentarily pained. "I could add more sports! How about this one from First Corinthians nine twenty-four. . . ." He cleared his throat dramatically. "*Do you not know that in a race all the runners run, but only one gets the prize? Run in such a way as to get the prize.*"

"Ah, classic." Miss O'Connor demonstrated how to slip the material through the machine and then traded places with Dad so he could give it a try. "But running a race is a little too spot-on. I love it when he tells me I have to get a 'third down on the fifty-yard line of life.' Like I have any idea what that means."

Dad began to hum the *Jungle Survivor* theme song again, looking all lit up inside.

When he held up his completed pants seam, Miss O'Connor congratulated him on his stellar sewing skills. They high-fived and laughed when they kinda missed. When Miss O'Connor went to use the bathroom, I gave Dad a goofy grin. "You and Miss O'Connor sure do laugh a lot together."

He grinned. "She's fun. One of my best friends."

I leaned in and lowered my voice. "But what if she could be more than a friend?"

The tips of Dad's ears turned pink. "You think I should ask out your teacher? Isn't that weird?"

I shrugged. "It seems weirder on paper. Miss O'Connor is awesome. And you two make each other laugh."

Dad looked like he was trying to work out a complicated math problem in his head. "There is no way she would go out with me. I've been completely friend-zoned. She knows all about my *irritable bowels*. . . ." He said the last two words with wide eyes just as Miss O'Connor came back in the room.

I didn't bother to tell him that after the Bachelors and Baskets picnic pretty much *everyone* knew about his irritable bowels.

Dad and Miss O'Connor continued to talk and joke as our costumes took form, but I could tell Dad was way more in his head. He stopped humming. He only told a few jokes. But I wasn't going to give up on this idea. Miss O'Connor made my dad happy, and that was my latest and greatest goal.

20

When Silence Isn't Golden

Around six the next night, there was furious knocking at the back door. Dad had just stepped out to attend a wedding rehearsal, and I was home alone and not really supposed to answer, but then I heard Bea's voice and some pretty intense knocking.

I flung the door wide and was face to face with Bea and a squirming, snot-nosed Julian. "You have to help me," she said, looking more desperate than I'd ever seen her before.

"Um, what exactly do you need help with?" I asked as Bea pushed past me into the kitchen.

"My mom had to take my granny to the hospital. She was having blurred vision and headaches, and my mom is worried that she might be having some kind of migraine or something?"

I patted Bea on the arm. "Oh no. Sorry about that. I'm sure she'll be just fine after your mom gets her to a doctor."

Bea nodded. "Yeah. You're probably right. But my dad is working tonight, so . . ."

I finally figured out what kind of help Bea needed. "So you're babysitting?"

Bea nodded, tears filling her eyes. "About ten seconds after Mom left, he tried to cut his own hair. I have no idea where he got scissors. I need an extra set of eyes."

I let out a slow breath and closed and locked the kitchen door. "Sure, no problem. We can tag-team it. I'm sure little Julian here will behave himself. Won't you, buddy?" I leaned close to Julian's round cherub face, and he reached out a chubby fist toward me. For a second I thought he was trying to hug me, but his sticky fingers curled around my dangly teardrop earring and he gave a yank.

"OW!" I yelled, backing away from the baby like he might be a wild animal.

Bea cringed. "You're going to want to remove those. Plus, any other part of your body you don't want yanked." She pointed to her hair, which was piled in a high and secure-looking bun on the top of her head.

I nodded and pulled an elastic band out of my pocket, twirling my hair into a ponytail before the little goober could grab it.

"Has he been fed and, like, changed and stuff?" I asked, sniffing the diaper region cautiously.

"Yeah," Bea said, patting a large bag she had slung over her other shoulder. "And I brought extra supplies."

"Okay, cool cool cool. Well . . ." We stood there sort of awkwardly in the kitchen. "What do we do now?"

Bea shrugged. "He's super boring when he isn't being super destructive."

"Those are our only choices?" I asked, eyeing a slimy string of drool escaping Julian's mouth.

"Boring, Destructive, and Asleep. Three modes."

"Let's stick with boring," I said.

We lugged the toddler into the living room, and I shot Dad a message explaining the situation. He didn't text back. Probably too busy telling people in the wedding party where to stand.

Bea pulled some cardboard kind of books out of her bag and sat next to Julian on the floor. She didn't even read the words in the books, she just pointed to things and said their names. Julian clapped his hands after every page. This didn't seem that hard.

"Hey," Bea said. "I know what will be fun. Let's play Bonk!" Bonk is where Bea and I take turns smacking each other in the head with pillows and yelling "Bonk!" and then falling over dramatically. Julian laughed hysterically. Every. Single. Time. The joke was evergreen. But then Bea got just a little too aggressive and whacked me so hard I went rolling off the back of the couch, and I smacked my head on the floor and saw stars for a second. I flew to my feet in a rage, grabbed the can of squeezy cheese we'd been snacking on, and chased her around the living room.

"I'm gonna cheese your face!" I screamed as Bea ducked behind the couch.

"You have to catch me first, slowpoke!" she yelled back.

There was a lot of running and squealing and laughing and ducking, and when we finally collapsed on the couch, breathing hard but un-cheesed, at first we didn't register the silence.

Silence, when you're watching a toddler, is bad.

Bea sat up at the exact same time that I did, and we looked at each other with wide eyes. "Where is he?" I asked at the same time that Bea jumped up and started calling, "Julian? Here, Julian!" like you would call a dog.

I followed a trail of fishy crackers down the hallway to my room, but I hadn't even pushed open the door yet when I heard Bea scream.

My feet took off in the direction of her cry, heart hammering in my chest. What was wrong? Was Julian hurt? Would I need to call an ambulance or 911 or something?

I stepped into the kitchen and instantly my feet slid out from under me. I landed on my back, staring up at the dusty light fixture. Bea was laughing, on the floor beside me, and

I realized she must have wiped out too. "What is going on?" I asked, sitting up and rubbing my now-doubly-sore head. "Why is the floor so . . ." And then I saw Julian.

He stood in the middle of the kitchen, holding the bottle of baby oil from his diaper bag. Or at least what was left of it. The contents of the almost-full bottle were now all over my kitchen floor and covering the little brat from head to toe. His hair was thick with it, and it was matted with some kind of white powder, which was joining the oil on the floor to make a paste.

"Julian, no!" Bea said, trying to scramble to her feet. It was like trying to walk with sticks of butter attached to your shoes.

"Oh my gosh. My dad is gonna—" Just then the back door opened and Dad walked in and promptly wiped out on the baby-butt-fresh floor.

Bea and I about died. We were laughing so hard, our heads were purple. Our stomachs hurt. Our faces were sore. My dad looked around at the greasy kitchen and the slimy baby and he started laughing too.

"What a little terror!" Bea said.

"At least he smells nice," I added, and then we burst into another round of giggles.

"It's all fun and games until somebody eats the diaper cream," Dad said, carefully lifting little Julian by the armpits and placing him gingerly in the sink. "I'll wash the baby. You wash the floor." He sighed. "This is gonna take a lot of baby shampoo."

Bea held up the empty bottle of No Tears Baby Shampoo, which set us off on a fresh round of giggles.

It was a major pain trying to get the entire contents of the diaper bag off the kitchen floor. Plus, after everything had been put right, Dad gave me a lecture about responsibility, even though it was pretty much all Julian's fault. But every time I thought about the three of us wiping out on the kitchen floor, I cracked up again. Sure, Bea's changing family meant some extra messes and responsibilities, but it wasn't all terrible. Changes could be fun . . . before they turned into a messy disaster, at least.

21

Brave Like Teddy

It was finally painting day. A whole Saturday to spend with my dad. Once we got the soft yellow paint on all the attic walls, it would be time for carpet, and then we could start moving my stuff up there. Dad whistled while he rolled the high parts and I carefully brushed around the edges. Potus sniffed everything and then curled into a ball near the window when he lost interest.

"Hey, Grace, what does the painter do when he gets cold?"

I squinted at the ceiling for a second. "He puts on another coat?"

"Awww, you've heard that one?" Dad said, leaning on his paint stick.

"No, you've just trained me well in the ways of puns. I am like a pun Jedi. You've made me join you on the dark side." I cracked up at myself, then realized that was exactly what my dad would do, which made me crack up more.

"So, you know I'm doing my research project on Teddy Roosevelt," I said, dipping my brush in the paint.

Dad chuckled. "How could I forget? Your research has gotten me my first reenacting job."

The more I'd studied Theodore Roosevelt, the more I'd accidentally studied Alice. I was so curious about her, a teenager growing up in the White House with a famous dad. I imagined it was a lot like being the preacher's kid in a small town. Everybody had ideas about what you should and shouldn't do. Everyone was all up in your business. Me and Alice had that in common.

"You know, Alice got herself in trouble a lot. Probably to get her dad's attention, since he'd gotten a new wife."

Dad laughed and turned to look at me. "Does this mean you plan to do a lot of bad stuff to get my attention?"

Oh, if he only knew all the bad stuff I'd done lately.

But I just smiled. "Does this mean you plan to get a new wife?"

He shrugged and went back to painting. "Let's not get ahead of ourselves."

Of course, this entire chat was making me think of Miss O'Connor and the spark I'd seen between her and my dad. I tried to steer the conversation in that direction.

"What if the person you like is right in front of you and you're just too chicken to ask her out?"

Dad turned to look at me. "Do you mean Gretchen?"

I groaned. "No, Dad, Miss O'Connor."

"Grace, I told you, Olivia just doesn't see me that way. I'm her pastor. And she's your teacher. And we're good friends. It would be weird."

"Stay right there." In a flash of inspiration, I dashed down the attic ladder and retrieved a book from my room.

I flipped to the page I was looking for and read the passage to my dad while he continued to paint: "*You would be hard pressed to find a more courageous president than Theodore Roosevelt. During his 1912 campaign against Taft, he was shot in the chest moments before he was scheduled to deliver a speech. The bullet was significantly slowed by the folded-up speech notes that were in his breast pocket; however, it was still lodged in his chest when he stood onstage and delivered his eighty-four-minute speech.*"

Dad stared at me. "I have no idea what I'm supposed to be getting from this story. What does this have to do with my dating life?"

"Dad. If Teddy Roosevelt, your alter ego, can deliver a whole speech with a bullet in his chest, you can do hard things too."

Dad scrunched up his nose. "You want me to give a speech?"

"What? No. I want you to be brave, like the president was. Sometimes being brave means staring adversity in the face. Sometimes it means being willing to look at people differently."

Dad rolled his eyes. He actually rolled his eyes teenager-style.

"How about we just finish in here and then you can help me paint my new office."

I flicked my brush in Dad's direction, sending a shower of paint across his shirt.

"Oh, you are gonna regret that, Giblet!" Dad said, flinging his arm around me and putting me in a headlock.

"P.U.! It stinks down here!" I squealed. Potus lifted his head and, in a burst of doggy energy, got up and tried to join our squabble, licking my face as I squirmed away from Dad.

It was all fun and games until Dad accidentally stepped in the paint tray and fell over, leaving one streaky footprint on the canvas drop cloth.

"Truce! Truce!" Dad called as I collapsed next to him, laughing.

I looked over at my dad's happy, paint-streaked face and smiled back. "Truce," I said. But I was talking about paint wars and not about the Miss O'Connor debate.

Bea and I met up at the library on Wednesday night to work on our famous-Americans projects. Bea came in, flushed and happy, and shook the rain off her jacket. "Sorry I'm late. Julian and I were stuck in this endless game of peekaboo."

"You aren't even late," I said, laughing. "You think if you aren't early, you're late."

"True," Bea said, smiling. "How's your project coming?"

"Great," I said. "But that is totally not what I want to talk about right now."

"Okay." Bea hesitantly sank into a chair without taking her eyes off me.

I shoved my pile of books aside. "I have a pretty good idea of who my dad should be dating. There's only one lady out there who makes him light up like a . . . like a . . . Hula-Hoop."

Bea raised her eyebrows. "Huh?"

"I have a Hula-Hoop that lights up when you spin it. It was the only thing I could think of that lights up." I shook my head. "Anyway, that's not the point."

"A Christmas tree. A lightbulb. A candle. A firework."

I gave Bea a pitying look. "Those are all kind of cliché. Anyway, back to the subject . . . I think we need to set my dad up with Miss O'Connor!"

"You want your dad to date our history teacher?" Bea asked, her voice going all high and squeaky.

I started ticking things off on my fingers. "She goes to our church, I've known her practically my whole life, she likes history and *Jungle Survivor*, and . . ." I lowered my voice to a whisper, even though the librarians weren't even around. "I think my dad really likes her, he just won't admit it."

Bea flipped through her book, but I could tell she wasn't even reading the words on the page. She looked at me, fist on her chin. "So, tell your dad to ask her out."

I sighed. "I tried that. He's in total denial."

"Well, I guess that's that. You promised yourself, and me, that you would stay out of his love life. No more scheming. No more breaking rules." She narrowed her eyes at me. "You promised."

I held up one finger. "I believe what I promised was that I would stop making my dad miserable with my schemes. This is completely different. I want to help him find happiness. What could be wrong with that?"

Bea groaned. "It's not going to make him *happy* when you keep messing with his dates."

I thought about that for a second. Bea was a little bit right. I had said I would stay out of things. But Miss O'Connor made my dad downright joyful. There had to be a nice, easy way we could give them a little push.

I held up one of my research books. Bea let out a breath that was like *Oh boy, here we go.*

"Did you know, Alice Roosevelt was always getting in the newspapers. She was super famous and popular."

Bea smirked. "And?"

"And her dad didn't love seeing her in the limelight. When he noticed an advertisement for a hospital charity event where you could pay five dollars to have Alice serve you tea, he freaked out. He sent her a letter that day demanding that she not show up for this charity event."

Bea looked confused but interested, so I went on. "Do you know what Alice did?"

Bea shook her head and muttered, "Why would I know that?"

"Alice poured tea at the event anyway. She ripped her father's letter up and told *him* it hadn't gotten to her in time."

"But your dad isn't going to write you a letter to tell you to stay out of his love life," Bea said.

"The point, my friend, is that it is better to ask for forgiveness than for permission."

Bea breathed out, a look of resignation crossing her face. "You know, you and rebel Alice have a lot in common."

I slammed the book shut. "A certain disregard for the rules? Yes."

Bea still looked worried. "And you want to help your dad and Miss O'Connor get together?"

"We will be secret Cupid rebels. We'll help my dad and

Miss O'Connor go on some dates so he'll cheer up and everything will be fine."

I jumped up and started pacing. "When's the next time we know for sure they'll be in the same room?" I went to my planner and started scanning the calendar and poked my finger at next weekend, my eyes bulging at Bea.

"What? What is it?" she asked, leaning toward the event scribbled on the very next weekend.

"The Seniors and Seniors banquet. I can work with that."

Bea pulled a bag of Skittles out of her backpack and dumped them on the table, trying to be quiet about it. "Fine," she said, pushing the reds and greens toward me. "Let's play Cupid. A nice, helpful, non-rule-breaking version of Cupid."

I laughed. "That is *so* not my style."

22

Seniors and Seniors

The Seniors and Seniors Spring Banquet is a fundraiser the high school youth group holds to raise money for their senior trip. They cater and serve all the senior citizens and other church members a banquet in the church fellowship hall. The high school kids are not known for their amazing cooking skills, or their choice of old-people-friendly music. It's pretty much a recipe for a headache and food poisoning. But this year the menu included a taco bar, and it's hard to mess up tacos. Plus, Bea and I had come up with a brilliant plan to help Dad and Miss O'Connor spend some quality time together. It was going to be amazing.

Bea didn't ride with Dad and me to the church, because I wanted her to get there ahead of time and set things up. It took some convincing, because she was worried that people would ask her what she was doing, but I told her to just say it was a surprise. She said I owed her about a million bags of Skittles.

When Dad and I walked up to the fellowship hall, there was a table right outside with two glass bowls on top, and a big poster that said ENTER TO WIN!

"What's this?" I asked Dad, even though I knew perfectly well what it was.

Dad leaned closer to the sign and read the fine print. *"This year's Seniors and Seniors banquet will feature one lucky couple as the Queen and King of the evening. They will get preferential seating (right by the taco bar!) and a delicious bonus dessert! Sign up here!"*

"Wow!" I said, enthusiastically writing my name on a slip of paper and dropping it into the bowl marked QUEEN. "I sure hope I win! This sounds awesome!"

Dad jabbed at the poster. "I don't think you're qualified. You probably have to be an actual senior."

I whispered conspiratorially, "It doesn't say that. Not specifically. It's a glaring loophole."

Dad laughed. "Well then, I hope you win, Giblet. You are royalty to me." He started to head into the banquet, but I grabbed his arm.

"Dad! You have to enter to be king!"

Dad pulled at his collar. "Uh, no thanks. Bad things happen to pastors who fancy themselves kings."

I groaned. "It's just for fun! And you get a bonus dessert! And if they make me queen, I would really want you to be the king."

Dad laughed. "Fine. But I'm only entering because I'm the unluckiest person I know. They'd have a better chance of pulling Grover Cleveland's name out of there than mine."

"You never know, Dad. Today might be your lucky day."

He signed his name with a flourish and added it to the king bowl.

Phase one of our plan was complete.

When we walked into the crowded fellowship hall, I spotted Bea right away and gave her a thumbs-up. She looked equal parts relieved and nervous. She really had no stomach for scheming. Luckily, her part of the plan was done.

Dad and I walked through the crowds of white-haired old ladies and bald-headed gentlemen. Dad shook hands and spoke extra loud so the old guys could hear him. I smiled at everyone, even the grannies who squeezed my cheeks and patted my hair. My eyes scanned the crowd for Miss O'Connor, but I didn't see her until we almost ran into each other at the taco bar.

"Hello, Grace!" Miss O'Connor said brightly. I had to blink a few times, because she looked amazing! She wore a sparkly red dress and black flats. Her hair was tamed in a low twisty kind of bun. She was glowing.

"Hi, Miss O'Connor," I said.

"Hey, isn't it supposed to be embarrassing when two ladies show up wearing the same dress?" she asked in a loudish whisper. I looked down at my own sparkly red dress and then cracked up. We looked like twins.

"Great minds think alike, I guess," I said.

We picked up our plates and faced the table full of taco fixings. But then her face crumpled and her shoulders started to shake.

My heart dropped. She was crying! I reached over and patted her shoulder. "What's wrong, Miss O'Connor?"

She sniffled loudly and then said, "I don't wanna *taco* 'bout it." Then she gave me that same wide-mouth smile my dad does when he's waiting for a laugh.

I cracked up, and quick as a whip added, "Sorry I was *jalapeño* business."

"It's *nacho* problem!" Miss O'Connor said, grinning. Then, giggling, we both started loading our plates. I crunched up two shells, because I like them salad-style so I can do my damage with a fork. Then I added meat and cheese. I skipped the lettuce because it was wilty and brown. Last, I added a big blob of salsa and a pile of jalapeño peppers. When I glanced over at Miss O'Connor's plate I nodded in appreciation. Her taco mountain was identical to mine.

"Is your dad here?" she asked, in a voice that sounded like it was trying to be casual.

"Yup, I left him right over there—" I stopped so abruptly, Miss O'Connor immediately looked up to see what had interrupted me. Dad was right where I'd left him. But Gretchen stood next to him, with her arm through his. *What's she doing here?* She didn't even go to our church. Dad must have invited her. I let out a frustrated breath but then shook my head. We still had our plan. It would be okay.

"Who's that talking to him?" Miss O'Connor asked. "She seems familiar."

"She was over the night you brought our fabric. Her name is Gretchen. I guess her and my dad are dating now."

She tilted her head and took a longer, more skeptical look at Gretchen. "Wait. I thought your dad was dating Rachel Watson? Isn't that what Miss Marge said in the bookstore a while back?"

I chuckled nervously. "He's been on a few dates lately."

She grabbed a big pile of napkins. "Pastor Davy is dating, huh? That's kind of weird."

I sighed. "You're telling me!"

She turned away from my dad and Gretchen and studied my face. "How are you doing with that? I know you two are super close."

I set my taco plate down at an empty table and Miss O'Connor sat opposite me. "I . . . I just want him to be happy, I guess. But I do think there's someone he might like better. If he gave her a chance."

I stared at my teacher's face, looking for the slightest flicker of emotion, but she kept it as smooth as a fresh jar of Skippy. "Grown-ups have to make their own decisions about these things, Grace" was all she said. I nodded, like I accepted this adult nonsense. But inside I was shaking my head. Some grown-ups, like my dad, needed a little push.

Bea came by and ate her tacos with Miss O'Connor and me and we both kept shooting nervous glances at my dad and Gretchen. She still hung off his arm, even while he tried to eat his tacos. And he wasn't smiling. She chattered away and looked perfect and everything, but he barely glanced at her. I had the feeling he wasn't all that happy that he'd invited her, and that gave me a little hope that phase two of our plan would be a success.

Bea nudged me when most everyone had finished their tacos and people were starting to mill around the fellowship hall. This was it. Phase two. Bea raised one eyebrow at me, and I gave her a quick nod. She disappeared into the kitchen, and I stood on a chair. Miss O'Connor stared at me with her mouth open, and after I clanged my glass with a spoon a few times everyone else stared at me too.

My knees felt like jelly as I waited for everyone to quiet down. "Hello, seniors! Thank you for coming out this evening and supporting our youth group. Let's give the seniors in high school a nice round of applause for putting this event on." The room erupted in polite applause and a few boys took rowdy bows. Pastor Steve looked completely puzzled. He was probably wondering why I was giving a speech at his event. But being the pastor's daughter does come with some perks.

"And now, I'd like to announce the queen and the king of the banquet. They will be enjoying a special dessert together as a lovely end to this evening."

I cleared my throat and looked everywhere but at Dad. I pulled a blank slip of paper out of my pocket, which I hoped everyone would assume I'd pulled out of the bowls by the door.

"The queen of the banquet is . . ." I pretended to read the name. "Miss Olivia O'Connor!" She stood up and did a perfect impression of a Disney princess, smiling and waving and bowing to her adoring fans.

I took a second slip of paper out of my pocket. "And the king of the banquet is . . . Davy Martin, our very own pastor, and my dad!" More clapping and my dad stood and nodded, a tightish smile on his face.

Bea emerged from the kitchen carrying a giant chocolate milkshake topped with whipped cream and a bright red cherry. She set it down in front of my dad and Miss O'Connor and added two straws with a flourish.

This was it. All they had to do was drink that milkshake

together, their heads all close, and sparks were sure to fly. I patted myself on the back for my genius. I was even better at creating dates than I was at sabotaging them.

And then Gretchen joined the royal table. Just like that. She pulled up a chair and took a drink off my dad's straw. Eeww. I had to get her out of there.

I walked up to the table and smiled a big cheesy smile at my dad. "See? Aren't you glad you entered? You totally won."

Dad raised an eyebrow at me, and I quickly tapped Gretchen on the shoulder. "Actually, Gretchen, you won something too." I pulled one of the slips of paper out of my pocket and pretended to read. "Gretchen is the winner of the Servant's Heart Award. This is a very special award that goes to the person with the most generous spirit and attitude of service. You get to help with the dishes."

Gretchen's mouth fell open, and Dad sprang to his feet. He snatched the paper out of my hand before I had time to react. He looked confused and then questioning.

"This is blank," he said. "Did you make up the Servant's Heart Award?" Then recognition dawned on his face. "Did you make up *this whole king and queen business*?" he asked in a panicked whisper.

"What? No. Dad. How could I make up a whole milk-shake? How could I make up two straws? This was all Youth Pastor Steve's idea." I waved at the spiky-haired guy from across the room and he waved back, still looking confused.

Dad dragged a hand down his face. "Olivia—Miss O'Connor. I am so sorry. I think I'd better get my little con artist home." I felt the plan falling to bits like my crunched-up taco shells. Why did my dad have to invite a date to this thing? And why couldn't Gretchen have just gone and washed dishes like a nice person? And why was my dad giving me that look like he was . . . disappointed in me? He hadn't even given that milkshake one little taste! Gretchen stuck her arm through his again, and I imagined peeling all of her red nail polish off. Bea waved at me and mouthed the word "Sorry!"

I hung my head and followed my dad out of the fellowship hall. Miss O'Connor shrugged and pulled the milkshake closer. She took a long drink and grinned to herself.

23

Little Brother

Bea called me up the next day and asked if I wanted to come over for dinner at her house. I hesitated, thinking about our babysitting adventures and then the tuna casserole night and wondering if I had the energy for that kind of chaos.

"Um, are you sure it's okay with your mom and everyone? I mean, isn't everybody pretty busy?"

Bea laughed. "Oh no! We scared you last time, didn't we? Things have calmed down around here, I promise."

I took a deep breath, and smiled, and said, "Great!" But I planned to escape as soon as things got wild.

Bea's house was noisy. And messy. But she was right, there wasn't thick panic in the air like the last time I'd come over. Her mom sang in the kitchen, stirring something that smelled amazing on the stove. Mr. Morrison lined up Cheerios on the high chair's tray, where Julian was gobbling them up, his drooly face smiling.

"Somebody needs a diaper change," Mr. Morrison said, lifting the baby out of the chair.

"I'll do it," Bea said.

"Wait, you're volunteering for the dirty work?" I whispered through gritted teeth.

Bea laughed. "He really likes it when I do it. I blow the best tummy raspberries, don't I, little guy?" She rubbed her nose with Julian's nose and I followed her to the toddler's room.

The sounds of the kitchen grew muffled in the background. "I am so glad you came over," she said, laying Julian down on the changing table. "We didn't even get a chance to talk after Operation: Milkshake-Two-Straws."

I groaned. "That was basically a disaster. Dad figured out I'd set up the whole thing and he was ticked about it. I got a whole lecture in the car about misleading the church members and stuff."

Bea gave me the side eye. "Did he notice that we were trying to get him and Miss O'Connor together?"

I shrugged. "What can I say? The guy's dense sometimes."

Bea smiled hugely, her face close to Julian's, but she was still talking to me. "That's that, then. There's nothing else we can do about it. I guess the secret Cupids are done."

I picked up a squashy blue dog from the floor. "Hey, it's Mr. Jiggles! I haven't seen him in forever!"

Bea smiled. "He lived in the attic for a while, but I decided to pass him on to my little brother."

Little brother?

For some reason, I had never thought of Julian as Bea's little brother. He was the new toddler in her family. He was her noisiest problem. He was a royal pain in the you-know-where. But somehow, I had forgotten that after the adoption he was also Bea's little brother. I looked at the squirmy kid with new interest.

Bea finished up the diaper change and then leaned over and blew spitty bubbles on her brother's tummy. He exploded in laughter so contagious we couldn't help but join him. Bea grabbed Mr. Jiggles and gave him a tight squeeze before tossing him in the crib in the corner.

"Does it stink having to share your parents with this guy?" I asked. Something curdled in my guts as I remembered Gretchen's hand on Dad's arm at the banquet. The secret Cupids could not possibly be done.

"Sometimes it stinks so bad I think the wallpaper might peel," Bea said, scooping up Julian and plopping down in the rocking chair. "Especially if he's had a bunch of prunes."

I laughed. "No, I mean doesn't it bug you?"

Bea shrugged. "It's weird. . . . At first I was so mad. I hated that my whole family got messed up and rearranged.

You know how I like things a certain way. And at times it seemed like I was the one making all the sacrifices. . . ." She smoothed Julian's hair. "But then we fell in love."

"Wait, what?" I asked.

"With Julian. We all did. Mom first, from like the second she held him. Me and Dad took a little longer. But now . . . I couldn't imagine our family without him."

I crossed my arms. "But he cries and poops and takes all your parents' time and attention and everything!"

"Yeah, but he also makes my mom sing lullabies. And my dad loves to bounce him on his knee while they watch baseball games together. And I read him the same three books every freaking night because those are the ones he likes best. He somehow makes all of us better."

"Beaeeeee," Julian said, smiling and pulling at one of her pigtails. "Beaeeee Beaeeee Beaeeee."

Bea gasped and her hand flew to her mouth. "That's right, buddy! I'm Bea! You said my name! Did you hear that? He said my name!"

We both erupted into giggles, as Julian, who was very proud of himself for mastering his sister's name, repeated it about eleventy billion times.

Bea flung him onto her hip and trotted him out to the kitchen and had him do his trick for both of her parents. You would have thought he'd composed his first symphony by the way they reacted. Their joy was pretty contagious.

And even though I noticed subtle changes in the way the family worked, everyone seemed happy. I watched Bea smiling and giving her little brother nose kisses, and I conceded that he hadn't, in fact, ruined the family. Maybe there was still hope for mine.

24

A Godly Man of God

Every March, the Springdale School District hosts a special Muffins with Mom event. Basically, your mom comes to school in the morning and sits at a sticky cafeteria table and eats a slightly stale blueberry muffin with you. Sometimes you give her a card and a paper flower you've made. It was all pretty silly, until I didn't have a mom to invite anymore.

During my very first Muffins Without Mom, my dad came to rescue me. He scooped me up and took me out to our favorite diner for a steaming plate of biscuits and gravy.

He was my knight in shining armor. He was Batman answering the Bat-Signal. He was a lifeguard saving a drowning girl.

So it became our tradition. Every year he rescues me from the dreaded event, swapping muffins for biscuits and gravy. It makes me feel like we're okay, just the two of us. That anytime I need a mom, Dad will do just fine.

I pulled on my rainbow-striped leggings and an over-sized unicorn sweatshirt and brushed my teeth methodically in the mirror.

The shower was running in Dad's bathroom, so at least he was up and getting ready. I banged on the bathroom door. "Dad! Don't forget Muffins with Mom is today!"

He stuck his head out the door, the shower still running. "Is that today?"

"Yes," I said, my voice getting all high-pitched and panicky.

"I know." He grinned, shutting the door in my face.

Jerk.

"Well, I'm going to walk to school with Bea," I said through the door.

"Okay, I'll be there at nine. With bells on."

"Please don't actually wear any bells," I said, and I was rewarded with a chuckle.

Bea and I walked at a brisk pace because even though spring was on its way, it was still chilly in the morning. I could see my breath come out in wispy puffs, and I tried to make sure my feet took two steps to every sidewalk square without stepping on the crack. Still didn't want to break anyone's back.

"So . . . today's that thing," Bea said, giving me a sideways glance.

"I know. Is your mom coming?"

"Yeah. I'm not sure I could get her to stay home. She's bringing the monster."

Bea said it like she was complaining, but the corner of her mouth twitched.

"He learned a new word yesterday," she said, covering her mouth with her hand. "Let's just say if *you* said it your dad would make you put a dollar in the swear jar."

My eyes widened and both of us laughed. Bea leaned in. "I hope Julian doesn't try out his new vocabulary at school. He's so embarrassing."

I think Bea hoped it would make me feel better when she complained about Julian and especially her mom, but it still made me miss my mom so bad my ears burned.

"Well, Dad will rescue me, like usual," I said, attempting to smile.

"You're lucky," Bea said, and then her face went slack and she tried to backtrack. "I mean, not lucky that your mom . . . I mean, just lucky your dad is so cool and . . . Sorry."

I smiled. "It's okay. I'll be fine."

After a brief half hour in homeroom, we were sent to the cafeteria to either eat a muffin with our mom, or watch other people do it. *What a horrible tradition.*

Bea said hi to her mom and they got in line. Bea's mom held a squirming Julian on her hip and other ladies kept coming up and cooing at him and fluffing his curly hair. Bea smiled so big her whole face glowed. She looked proud and really, really happy. It made me wanna pinch her a little bit, to be honest.

I pulled my notebook from my backpack and decided I would ignore everyone until my dad arrived. I drew a pile of biscuits in my notebook, smothered with some peppery Southern gravy. And at the top of the page I wrote, "Biscuits and Gravy beats Muffins any day!"

But as the minute hand on the cafeteria clock ticked on and on and my dad hadn't made his appearance, I started to get a twitchy feeling in my feet. I was surrounded by kids and moms and muffins and it squeezed me, suffocating me. I needed to get out of there. I stood up and flung my backpack over one shoulder and marched toward the bathrooms.

"Grace?" Miss O'Connor touched my shoulder and stopped me midmarch.

"Oh, hey," I said, trying to step around her.

"Um, your dad couldn't make it. He had an emergency."

I turned around to face her. "What? What kind of emergency?" My heart pumped triple-time as I remembered the day of Mom's accident. I pictured Dad on the ambulance stretcher and I couldn't move air in my lungs. *Not again. I can't live through that again.*

Miss O'Connor read the distress on my face and quickly

put her arm around me. "Your dad's okay. He just had to go visit someone at the hospital. It had to be now, you know?"

Someone from our church was hurt enough or sick enough or just plain old enough that they needed the pastor to come pray with them in the hospital. I felt my chest loosen, but only slightly. My hands were shaky. I thought about whoever it was and sent up my own prayer for them, and for the family they might be leaving behind.

This was part of being a pastor's daughter. You had to share your dad when duty called, but it didn't mean you had to like it.

Sighing, I resigned myself to Muffins with Mom without the other half of Team Gravy.

I hated muffins.

I nodded to Miss O'Connor and tried to squirm out from under her arm to go hide in the bathroom, but she snagged my backpack. "Hey, can I hang out with you? I could really go for a muffin about now."

"Don't you have class?"

"All the teachers are in here," she said, gesturing around the crowded cafeteria.

I shrugged. Fine. If she wanted to share in my misery, that was just great.

We got into the muffin line, which was much shorter now, and I tried to glance over at her without her noticing.

She was dressed for school, in a long dress printed with kittens playing with balls of yarn. Her hair bounced wild and curly, and her cat-eye glasses hung around her neck on a chain. Overall, she looked eccentric, but then I glanced down at my unicorn sweater and rainbow leggings and figured we made an excellent pair. In fact, if I had to be stuck at this thing with anyone besides Dad, I'd probably want it to be Miss O'Connor.

We reached for the same chocolate chip muffin at the same time and then laughed. "You take it. It's the last one," Miss O'Connor said.

"No, you can have it. I'll take . . . this poppy seed one."

Miss O'Connor leaned close to my ear. "Nobody likes the poppy seed ones. How 'bout we just split this?"

I smiled and nodded.

We carried our muffin and a stack of napkins to the only empty end of a long cafeteria table. For a second, I worried that kids would make fun of me for sitting with a teacher, but everyone liked Miss O'Connor and I guessed I didn't really care what they said anyway.

"How's your famous-American research going?" Miss O'Connor asked, plopping down across from me.

"Great!" I said. "Did you know that Teddy Roosevelt built the Panama Canal *and* went on an African safari *and* won the Nobel Peace Prize *and* went on a river expedition in Brazil for forty-eight days!" I could feel my cheeks pinking up. *Tone it down, nerd.*

But Miss O'Connor hung on my every word, nodding, chewing manically on a bite of muffin. "Wow! That's an impressive amount of research you've done already!"

I shrugged. "I like him. Definitely our coolest president."

"I could not agree more." Miss O'Connor smiled, her eyes crinkling around the edges. She smelled like muffins and flowers. "And have you come across much about Edith and the children? They were quite fascinating as well."

I scrunched up my nose. "Alice is great. But so far, I haven't found a shred of evidence that Edith was even the tiniest bit fascinating. In fact, it seems to me that she stole Alice's father away from her." I stared at my chunk of muffin. The room full of mothers was suffocating again.

Miss O'Connor's voice was soft. "Ah, maybe you need to dig deeper. See, it was Edith who put the family back together after Teddy and Alice had suffered so much."

I gulped. Just like me and Dad had suffered so much. I felt my knee go bouncy under the table and I wanted to bolt more than ever. I tucked this little bit of information away to research later.

"So . . . this event must be kinda hard," Miss O'Connor said, carefully chewing her last bite of muffin.

"Yeah. I pretty much hate it. But Dad usually saves me."

"I know. He was so worried when he called me. He wanted to make sure you didn't have to sit here alone."

I smiled a half smile. "I don't even think he realizes how much he depends on you for stuff."

Miss O'Connor blushed. "We're good friends. He's a good man. A good pastor. He is a godly man of God who is my pastor." She stumbled over her words and she tried to look everywhere else but at me. I studied her face, cheeks pink and eyes darting around the crowded cafeteria.

Aha! I was right! She likes him!

She's totally crushing on my dad!

I knew it!

"So, how come you never got married?" I asked, finishing off my half of the muffin.

Miss O'Connor smiled. "Never met the right guy, I guess."

"What about a good man, who is a good pastor, who is a godly man of God who is your pastor?" A wicked grin stole across my face.

"What? No. I mean, I've never thought about your dad that way."

"Never?"

She looked down at the table. "You aren't really supposed to go around having crushes on your pastor. That is deranged. But I do like his sense of humor. He's pretty funny."

"He is. And he's brilliant. Plus, you guys like the same

stuff." I couldn't help but notice that Miss O'Connor and I liked a lot of the same stuff too. Quirky clothes and sewing and taco mountains and history. I was starting to see Miss O'Connor as more than just my teacher and Dad's friend. She was my friend too.

"There was this one time, last summer at the church's bonfire night . . ." Miss O'Connor's face got all dreamy, and I gave her an encouraging nod. "We sat next to each other, talking and laughing. He toasted my marshmallows for me, extra burnt, just how I like them."

"Then what happened?" I asked.

She shrugged. "Nothing. I thought there was . . . I don't know . . . a spark or something? But then the next day we were back to being buddies."

Her eyes looked sad. "Look, I'm not going to argue with you that your dad is great. But he's never indicated he wanted to date me."

These two kids liked each other and both of them thought they had no chance. I felt a bubble of hope rising in my chest. I could help them finally be honest with each other.

"And what about that woman he's seeing?" Miss O'Connor asked.

I twirled my hair around my finger. "Nobody he's gone out with has ever made him laugh like you do. Or knows all about how Andrew Jackson taught his pet parrot to curse.

Or watches *Jungle Survivor* and roots for people to eat all their food on the first day like we do."

She laughed. "Well, that's very specific criterion."

I smiled. "It really is."

She stood up, shaking crumbs off her dress. "If only we could re-create the magic of the melty marshmallows . . ."

I'll have to work on that.

Miss O'Connor hadn't just helped out Dad by keeping me company among the muffins and moms. It was nice to sit across from her, to talk to her, and to listen to her. She made me feel warm and full, like I'd just polished off a giant bowl of macaroni and cheese. Was it possible that finding the right person for Dad could actually make me happier too?

25

May the Best Lady Win

Dad left me Apology Biscuits and Gravy every morning for the next few days. I wasn't even mad at him for standing me up, but I could tell he felt awful about it. I was just happy that Saturday we were knocking the Truman Library off our presidential bucket list, and that meant junk food and car tunes. Maybe I'd even have a chance to talk to Dad about Miss O'Connor.

He groaned when I clicked his light on, but I managed to get him up and dressed and ready to go within thirty minutes, with the help of a full pot of coffee. We stopped for breakfast sandwiches before we got out on the highway and then we were in full-out road trip mode.

I flipped through the radio stations, while Dad set the GPS at the first stoplight out of town. "Two hours and fourteen minutes to Independence," he said when he'd entered the address.

I bounced on my seat. "This will be awesome." More than two hours of Team Gravy time. We couldn't wait to see the exhibit "Saving the White House, Truman's Extreme Makeover." Harry Truman had massively overhauled the White House after a piano fell through the second floor.

To make the drive go by faster, Dad and I played a game of US Presidential Trivia. I had a battered book of questions and answers we'd used for this very game on many occasions, but we still managed to trip each other up once in a while.

"Who is the only president to be elected in two nonconsecutive terms?" I asked, taking a long sip of my Dr Pepper.

"Who is Grover Cleveland?" Dad answered. He wiggled his eyebrows at me, because for some reason he found the name Grover hilarious.

"Correct, but I'm deducting points for answering the question in the form of a question. This isn't *Jeopardy!*"

"Boo. Bad form. Give me another one."

"Okay. What three presidents have died on the Fourth of July?"

"A three-part question. I like it. Okay, the first one was John Adams. I know that."

"Correct."

"Thomas Jefferson."

"Correct."

"And . . . are you getting hungry? Should we stop for lunch?"

"Dad! We just ate breakfast! You don't know it, do you?"

"I know it! I'm just teasing you. I totally know it."

"Well?"

"Bill Clinton?"

"BEEEEEP." I made a loud buzzer noise, and Dad pretended to swerve the car in shock. "I am pretty sure Clinton is still alive."

"Are you sure? Let me see the book."

We laughed and I told him the correct answer, which was James Monroe.

"Who cares about death dates anyway? Did you know that Calvin Coolidge was *born* on the Fourth of July?"

"Yes, I knew that. You know who else would've? Miss O'Connor." I was careful not to look over at him.

Dad glanced at me out of the corner of his eye. "Yeah, she probably would have. But would she know that Teddy Roosevelt was blind in one eye from a boxing injury?"

"Yeah, I'm guessing she would. She loves this stuff."

I tried to read the expression on Dad's face, but it stayed strangely unreadable.

"You really like Miss O'Connor, huh? She's a pretty good teacher?"

I flipped through my book. This was it. Time to give him the hard sell.

"She's more than my teacher, isn't she? I mean, you don't call or text just any old teacher with a sewing emergency. Or a muffin crisis."

"I guess we do depend on her a lot. She's a good old gal." Dad didn't take his eyes off the road. *A good old gal? That sounds like something you'd say about your grandma!* Not exactly the reaction I hoped for.

"I wonder why she never got married," I said, trying again.

"Maybe she doesn't want to. It's not a life goal for everyone."

"It is for you."

"Hey now . . ." He glanced over at me.

I sighed. Dad was lonely and it was time for him to find someone. But it had to be the *right* someone.

"But I don't think that's why Miss O'Connor never got married. I mean, I think she would get married . . . if she met the perfect person."

"Well, so would I. If I met the perfect person."

Like a person who loves history trivia and fixing up old cars and has a healthy disdain for the youth pastor? That kind of perfect?

Dad's fingers bounced on the steering wheel. "As a matter of fact, I wanted to talk to you about something."

"What?" My heart skipped a beat. Maybe he'd read my mind. Maybe he'd decided to ask Miss O'Connor out at last!

"I've been seeing a bit more of Gretchen. Remember Gretchen?" He turned to face me, smiling crookedly.

My face fell. "Gretchen from the Seniors and Seniors banquet? Gretchen the boring auditor? Gretchen who put frogs in your backpack and stole your paper route money?"

"Now, that's not a flattering description, but yes. You liked her, right?"

I stared out the window. I wanted Dad to be happy. And Gretchen was . . . fine.

I shrugged. "She's okay. What do you mean you've been seeing more of her?"

"She has a client close to the town square, a block from the church, and we've met up for lunch a few times this month."

"A few times?" *Dad's going out on dates while I go to school?* My mouth went dry and I felt betrayed. "What about Miss O'Connor?"

He looked confused. "What about her?"

"You should ask her out. She's, like, your best friend."

Dad's face softened. "Yes, she is. But that's kind of the reason I can't go asking her out. It would make things weird. Plus, she's your teacher—"

"That doesn't bother me," I interrupted.

"Well, it doesn't help make things less awkward." Dad's face softened. "There was a moment . . . last summer. We were toasting marshmallows at the church's bonfire night. She said she felt terrible about impaling the marshmallows and then roasting them over a fire. She did these high-pitched voices. . . . I dunno, it made me laugh. She always makes me laugh . . . and I thought maybe she and I . . ."

Bingo! Bonfire night again! Dad had felt it too!

"I thought there was *something*. But then I remembered she is a member of my church and your teacher and I see her all over town, so if things went wrong . . . I just don't want to mess up what me and you and Olivia have. Okay?"

We drove in silence for the last hundred miles. I thought about how complicated this whole dating thing was. Grown-ups needed to come up with a new system.

When we pulled into the parking lot at the Harry S. Truman Presidential Library and Museum, Dad and I sat in the truck for a few more minutes. Finally, he turned to me. "It's fine, isn't it? Me dating Gretchen? I hoped you'd be okay with it."

"Gretchen's all right, Dad," I said, stowing the trivia book. "She's just no Miss O'Connor."

Dad ruffled my hair, like I hate. "You don't get to pick who I date, Giblet. Unless we can make a deal: You can select my dates if I can choose yours. In five years, when you're allowed to date."

I rolled my eyes. "No deal."

"Come on. I'd pick strapping young lads. Sammy Franklin has been volunteering at church a lot this year."

"Ugh. The glue-eater? No."

"Fine, then let me choose my own dates. M'kay?"

"If you insist," I said. "Now let's go learn about old Give 'em Heck Harry." I stepped out of the car and stretched my legs, taking in the long white building sitting up on the hill.

Dad might be dating Gretchen, but I wasn't about to give up on Miss O'Connor. I liked her, and I liked how happy Dad was when she was around. He just needed to see her in a different light. Maybe by bonfire light.

26

Spread S'more Love

"Everything looks fine under here. Tell me the noise your dad's truck was making again?" Miss O'Connor's voice was muffled by the truck's hood.

I pretended to thoughtfully inspect the ceiling of the garage. "Um, I think he said a clunking? Or maybe a chugging?"

Miss O'Connor reappeared, a grease streak on her nose. "A chugging? It's a diesel engine. It's supposed to chug."

I shrugged. "Hmm. I guess you'll have to talk to him about it. He'll be home soon. Would you like to come inside for some hot cocoa?" It was chilly in the garage, even though the sun shone brightly outside. Miss O'Connor smiled.

"That sounds wonderful."

The truth was, my dad's truck was fine. The extra truth was that Bea and I had concocted another plan to try to get Miss O'Connor and Dad together. The secret was in the s'mores. Both Dad and Miss O'Connor had mentioned the church bonfire night and the connection they'd felt. If we could just re-create that melty marshmallow goodness, maybe they would both confess how they were feeling.

Miss O'Connor followed me inside, and I ushered her into the downstairs bathroom. "You have some grease on your face. You might wanna clean up a bit."

"Oh, thanks," she said, closing the door behind her.

"I'm gonna just go fix your hot cocoa," I said, but instead I went to check on Bea and Dad. She had told him she had some questions about the Bible, and that had pretty much kept him out of my way for the last hour. Long enough to get Miss O'Connor over here and set everything up.

I heard Bea ask Dad, "So that Zacchaeus. I hear he was a wee little man. . . . Do you think that was literal or figurative?" I stuck my head in the kitchen and gave Bea a thumbs-up and she looked relieved. "Uh, never mind, Pastor Davy. I think you've done a wonderful job of explaining stuff to me today."

"Anytime, Bea. I love to sit down with a young person and talk through all their questions. I think it's great that you take your faith so seriously." Bea's ears turned bright red as Dad stood up and stretched. "Hey," he said, his voice taking on that mischievous tone. "What's the different between Jesus and a pizza?"

Bea looked helpless. "Probably a lot of things?"

"Jesus can't be topped." Dad cracked up and repeated "Can't be topped!" to himself.

"Hilarious, Dad. Why don't you make us some hot cocoa?" I said, grabbing Bea by the arm and leading her out of the kitchen toward the living room.

"You got it," Dad called, and then I heard him repeat, "Can't be topped!"

The living room glowed warmly. I'd turned the lights off and lit candles all around. Logs were stacked in the hearth, just waiting for fire. I'd scattered pillows and cozy blankets on the floor near the fireplace and placed a huge tray piled high with all the s'mores fixings in the center.

"Last thing," Bea whispered. She pressed Play on her iPad and soft classical guitar music came through the Blue-tooth speaker. We grinned and high-fived, because this just had to work.

"I'll go get Miss O'Connor," I said. "Get my dad to light the fire, and then stall him."

Bea groaned. "I've already asked him to explain the en-tire Book of Deuteronomy. I don't know if I can listen to him anymore."

I patted her arm. "You're doing great, friend. Thanks for helping me."

"Only because this is very sweet, and I can't see you

getting in trouble for lighting a few candles and setting out some snacks."

"Exactly. Now to make sparks fly."

I knocked on the bathroom door, and Miss O'Connor's voice sounded thin and wispy.

"Are you okay in there?" I asked through the door.

"Mm-hmm. I just have a headache. I was looking for some aspirin."

"Look behind the mirror, in the medicine cabinet," I said.

A few seconds later, the door opened, and Miss O'Connor emerged. The grease was gone from her nose, and her face looked pink and pretty, like she'd splashed it with cold water.

"The hot cocoa is in the living room," I said, bouncing on my heels.

"Oh, Grace. That sounds so nice, but I think I might head home now."

"No!" I said, so briskly that Miss O'Connor jumped.

"I just mean . . . we want to say thank you for coming over to take a look at Dad's truck. That was really nice of you. You earned this hot cocoa."

I took her hand and led her into the candlelit living room. Dad stood by the hearth with two mugs of cocoa, and Bea held the third.

"Olivia!" Dad said, his face breaking into a wide grin. "I didn't even know you were here!"

Miss O'Connor looked confused, but then she noticed the candles, the fire roaring in the fireplace, and the s'mores fixings on the tray.

She glanced at me. "Grace mentioned you'd heard your truck make a funny sound, so I came to check it out." Miss O'Connor's voice had a dreamy sound to it, like she was about to fall asleep. Maybe that's what people sound like when they fall in love?

Dad took a few steps toward her still holding the steaming mug of cocoa. "I . . . don't actually know what to say. I just came into the living room, and it was all candles and mood music. I promise I didn't have anything to do with this."

"Dad!" I whispered through gritted teeth. "I think what you meant to say is 'Thank you for coming over here on a Saturday to look at my old junker truck.'"

He gave me a stern look, but there was a sparkle behind his eye. He was going to pretend to be mad about this, but I could tell he wasn't. He and Miss O'Connor were in a serious eyeball lock. They both had dreamy, dizzy looks on their faces. Miss O'Connor was even swaying a little bit to the music, like she wanted to dance.

"Grace is right. Thank you for coming to look at my truck. Did you find anything wrong with it?" Dad asked.

"No, everything looked perfectly fine," Miss O'Connor answered.

"That's odd," Dad said, cocking his head at me. "At least you didn't cut my brake lines," he muttered, loud enough for only me to hear.

But then he looked around the room, and back at Miss O'Connor.

"This sort of reminds me of—" Dad started.

"—bonfire night, last summer," Miss O'Connor finished. Her eyes looked glassy, but she had a big smile on her face.

Yes. Exactly! This was totally going to work. These two had just needed a little push in the direction of s'mores, and by the end of the night they would be planning their next date.

"There's a cozy fire over there, and marshmallows that need toasting. I think me and Bea will just leave you two alone."

Miss O'Connor took two steps toward us, and at first I thought maybe she'd give me and Dad a hug. Instead, her hands flew to her mouth, but it was too late. She barfed all over both of us.

27

No Kindness Is Ever Wasted

I'd never seen Bea leave our house in such a hurry. "I don't do puke" was the last thing she said before she sped out the door. Me and Dad helped Miss O'Connor to the couch. She kept repeating, "I'm so sorry. I'm soooo sorry. I ruined s'mores night. . . ."

"There's nothing to apologize for. Is there someone we can call for you? Your parents or a special friend?" Dad's face went red, like he couldn't even say the word *boyfriend*.

Miss O'Connor's face blanched pasty white, despite her rosy glow earlier, which I realized was probably a fever. I got her a wet washcloth, and she held it to her head. "No. There isn't anyone to call."

Dad sprang into action. "I'll get everything cleaned up. Are you warm enough? Do you need another blanket? How about some tea?"

Miss O'Connor smiled weakly, but her eyes never left his face. "Tea sounds wonderful, thanks."

Dad started cleaning up the puke with a damp towel, and I ran into the kitchen to help get things ready. *Why did this have to happen? Why did Miss O'Connor have to get sick?* Just when it seemed like everything was falling into place, she went and puked on his shoes. Things were getting desperate.

Dad joined me in the kitchen and fumbled around, looking first for a clean mug, and then for the tea bags. While he did that, I found a wooden tray Mom used to bring me toast and tea when I was sick. I spread a red-checked napkin over it and added a small cup of water with a few daffodils from the windowsill. It was just starting to show signs of spring outside, and I'd cut the blooms yesterday to brighten up the kitchen. I wanted everything to be perfect for Miss O'Connor, so onto the tray they went.

Dad turned around, gripping the hot tea, and eyed the tray skeptically. "What's all that for?"

I groaned. "Dad, come on. Just try to be nice."

"What do you mean, 'try to be nice'? I am nice. I'm always nice. I mean, I'm letting the lady lie on my couch after she puked all over me. . . ."

"Let's try to forget all about that. Think about right before she puked. Were you catching any feelings?"

"Grace, I'm not having this conversation with you. I've already told you, I'm dating Gretchen. I know you like Olivia better." He chuckled. "Re-creating bonfire night was a sly move."

My heart sank. He'd figured out my entire plan . . . and laughed at it like it was babyish.

"You know you can't make grown-ups fall in love by having them share a milkshake or toast a marshmallow, don't you?"

"I never said anything about falling in love. I just thought maybe you could see each other differently."

Dad picked up the tray, to which I'd added two slices of toast on a flowered plate, and walked two steps toward our recovering barfer.

"Olivia and I are just friends. Getting us to eat s'mores won't change that, Grace." His voice softened. "It was a thoughtful thing you did. You went to a lot of trouble to set all this up. I'm just telling you, it won't work." He turned on his heels and walked to the living room.

I stood at the kitchen door and listened to them talking. Miss O'Connor's voice was too low to hear, but Dad said something about "Grace's idea." I fumed. Why couldn't he just try? Be honest about his feelings? Why did he have to shut Miss O'Connor down before he'd even given her a chance?

And then the doorbell rang.

Maybe Bea was back for her iPad? Or maybe we'd ordered a pizza we'd forgotten about? But I had a sinking feeling in the pit of my stomach it was neither of those things.

I walked into the living room just as Dad opened the door. Gretchen stood on the porch, holding two coffees in paper cups. She grinned from ear to ear. "Coffee delivery!" she said, stepping into the living room.

"Gretchen, I didn't know you were coming over." Dad glanced at the other woman stretched out on his couch.

"I was in the area, and I . . . Oh, is this a bad time?" Her eyes glanced around at the flickering candles and then narrowed at Miss O'Connor.

Dad fumbled to flick on the overhead light. "Well, yes and no. You remember Grace's teacher, Miss O'Connor? She came over to look at my truck, but then she got ill, and I didn't want to send her home alone."

"Ah, so you're playing Florence Nightingale. Be careful, patients tend to fall in love with their nurses." She threw back her head and laughed, but Miss O'Connor and Dad both looked suddenly fidgety.

"Here, soy latte, for you." Gretchen handed Dad the lidded cup.

I sat at the end of the couch where Miss O'Connor's feet were. "Dad likes caramel macchiatos."

"Grace, that's not polite," Dad whispered.

"Oh, I'm sorry. I just got you what I always get." For the first time, Gretchen looked slightly uncomfortable.

"It was sweet of you to think of me and bring me coffee. Thank you so much."

Miss O'Connor sat up, touching her forehead and grimacing. "I should go home. You all have a whole Saturday evening ahead of you, and I need a nap."

I said, "No, stay," at the same time Gretchen said, "Bye, feel better!"

Dad cleared his throat. "Olivia, you're welcome to stay here until you're one hundred percent again."

"No thank you. I'll get my coat." She swayed on her feet dizzily and I ran to the front closet to get her jacket. My whole brilliant plan had crashed and burned and somehow Gretchen had weaseled her way into our Saturday.

Dad and Gretchen laughed, their heads close together. Making fun of me, no doubt. He'd probably told her all about how I'd tried to set him up with my teacher, like I was some clueless kid who didn't even know how love worked. I couldn't help but notice Gretchen hadn't bothered to bring a paper cup for me. I enjoy a mocha just as much as the next girl. I glared at her perfect hair and her stylish back as I thrust the coat at Miss O'Connor.

"Thanks for the tea and toast." She smiled weakly at me. "And for all the rest." She winked, but winced as if it would split her head in two.

"Will I see you at church on Sunday?" Dad said, opening the door for her.

"Guess it depends on if I'm still barfing," Miss O'Connor answered sweetly.

Gretchen recoiled, and it looked like it took everything in her power to not cover her mouth and nose until Miss O'Connor left. She would probably whip out the Lysol and spray the couch and hallway as soon as Miss O'Connor was out the door.

"Take care of yourself," Gretchen said through gritted teeth. She put her arm around Dad's shoulders and smiled, but it didn't look like she was breathing.

"I always do," Miss O'Connor said, with her back to us. She was already halfway down the sidewalk.

"Dad, I can't believe you let her go home! She's sick! She needs us!"

Gretchen swept over to the couch but decided not to sit. "She needs to rest. Plus, your dad doesn't want to wait on her hand and foot all evening."

Dad stared at the closed front door, and I saw something flicker across his face, but then he took a drink of his soy latte and swallowed with some difficulty.

"Kindness is never wasted," he said softly.

"What's that?" Gretchen didn't glance up from her phone.

"My dad always says, 'No kindness is ever wasted.'"

He pulled me into a side hug.

"Well, I, for one, don't enjoy cleaning up other people's vomit. Not my favorite way to spend a Saturday. Grace, why don't you take this and go to a movie?" She pressed a crisp twenty-dollar bill into my hand.

Did she think she could just buy me off? Shoo me away? And the worst part was, Dad didn't say a thing to stop me.

I put on my coat as Gretchen and Dad chatted in low voices. The other half of Team Gravy didn't even notice when I left.

28

Dodgeball with Ducks

I went to the one place that always helps my brain work through things when I'm super mad. The duck pond.

Evening was settling in as the ducks swam in lazy circles around the murky pond. The water was as dark as my heart. I picked up an acorn off the ground and flung it, accidentally hitting a ducky square in the tail feathers. It gave a disgruntled squawk before moving out of range.

How could this have happened? Everything had blown up in my face. Dad was more interested in Gretchen than in Miss O'Connor. And mood music and a pile of s'mores hadn't even distracted him for ten minutes. I chucked another acorn, but luckily this time I didn't hit any feathered friends.

After my mom died, I knew everything was broken. Our lives would never be happy again, and I would always be missing something. Dad tried so hard to fix everything.

On my first birthday without Mom, he planned a "spa day" at home, complete with facials and mani-pedis. We wore towels on our heads and green masks on our faces. He made me believe as long as we had each other, we didn't need anyone else.

But then he'd gone and decided that wasn't true! When pushy Miss Donna and Miss Marge mentioned he should meet a nice lady, he didn't say, "No, me and my daughter are perfectly fine, thank you." He wasn't as happy with Team Gravy as he'd led me to believe. He wanted more.

And recently I'd been feeling like I wouldn't hate having a stepmom around. As long as it was the right one. As long as it was someone who wouldn't mess us up. But Gretchen had just done what I'd feared the most. She'd sent me away. And Dad was too busy staring into her sparkly eyes to even notice.

I chucked another nut.

"Knew you'd be here." My breath hitched, and I snapped my head toward the sound of his voice.

Dad sat down, then picked a few acorns off the ground and handed them to me. "Playing dodgeball with the ducks again?"

"How did you know where I went?" I asked. Even though I was secretly pleased that Dad had found me, I had to keep reminding myself that I was angry with him. He was the one who was breaking up the team.

Dad studied an acorn in his hand. "Remember the time when you were five and you told us you wanted to run away from home?"

I had a flash of memory. I was stuffing my Hello Kitty backpack with a box of graham crackers and a jar of peanut butter.

"You were so mad at me, you told me you wanted to live at the park. You strung a blanket up right over there." He pointed underneath a platform on the play structure, and I could faintly remember sitting in my makeshift tent, eating my graham crackers and peanut butter and feeling angry at my dad.

"Why did I want to run away?" Whatever it was, it couldn't have been worse than getting handed twenty dollars and being told to get lost.

"You and I had been working on a jigsaw puzzle for weeks. It was of the White House. Which means all the pieces were basically white. It was some serious parental misjudgment to buy it for you in the first place. Some would say I had set you up for failure."

I remembered squinting at the jagged white pieces, holding them up to the light. Trying over and over again to make them fit. "You finished the puzzle without me. When I was sleeping." My footie pajamas had made a pattering sound all the way down the stairs. I'd stopped when I'd reached the living room and stared at the puzzle, completely finished.

Dad hung his head. "I thought it would make you happy! You were getting so frustrated with it. I stayed up half the night to surprise you."

"And I took one look and declared I was moving out," I said, smiling a little bit at my dramatic kindergarten self.

"I wanted to try to stop you. I thought about locking you in your room! Of course, Mom knew best. She said to let you have some space. But we definitely followed you in the car." Dad laughed, his eyes crinkled at the memory. "We sat here and watched you until it started to get dark. I wanted to go over and beg your forgiveness and buy you ice cream and fix everything, but instead we waited. And when the first streetlights came on you packed up your bag and headed home."

"You were here the whole time?" I asked, my voice cracking.

"Giblet, I would've camped out here all night. I would've crossed mountains and oceans. I would've done that entire impossible jigsaw puzzle again. All I wanted was for you to forgive me and to come home. As far as I could remember, that was the last time you were ever truly angry at me. So, tonight, after I sat there and drank that disgusting coffee like a nincompoop while my girlfriend scrolled Twitter, I hoped you'd be camped out here, waiting for me."

"What about Gretchen? She seemed to have some plans today that did not involve me." I launched an acorn.

Dad rubbed the back of his neck. "I told her I needed to be with my daughter tonight, the other half of my team. And I told her that we had plans, just me and you."

"What kind of plans?" I asked, finally looking up into my dad's face.

"I was thinking we should get a completely white jig-saw puzzle and attempt to put it together!" We laughed and Dad put his arm around me. "I don't care what we do, as long as I'm with you."

It was finally beginning to feel like spring, and nobody was happier about this than Potus. Anytime Dad or I walked past his leash, hanging by the door, he ran in circles, beg-ging for a walk.

"All right, Potus. I'll take you. Just hold on." I left Dad a note and put on a jacket, and then the two of us headed out into the sunshine.

Potus liked to stop and smell every leaf and blade of grass and that was fine with me because my mind was rac-ing, even if my feet weren't.

My dad.

Team Gravy.

Miss O'Connor.

Gretchen.

What was the right thing to do here? Was I supposed to just sit back and let Dad continue to date Gretchen, when I knew (even if he didn't) that Miss O'Connor was the right lady for him?

I kicked a rock and followed Potus down the street. The sky was a brilliant blue, and spring flowers were popping up in garden beds and around mailboxes. Potus cocked his head at every bird that called to its buddies, and we passed several neighbors who were all out trying to soak up the sunshine.

I kept thinking about that White House puzzle. I had assumed me and Dad were gonna finish that thing together. It was our special project, and I had thought we were a team. But then, BAM, he went and finished it without me. And somehow the picture didn't look exactly like I had thought it would.

And now Dad was doing it again. I had a good idea what the last piece of our family's puzzle should be, and what the final picture should look like, but he'd gone and crammed in a wrong last piece!

Potus lifted his head and let the warm breeze ruffle his ears. "Dad should be with Miss O'Connor. She's the last piece of our puzzle." Potus looked at me solemnly and I took that as a *Yes, Grace. I agree with you completely.* Then he spotted a butterfly and practically yanked me off my feet chasing it. We slowed back down to a normal walking pace after a few steps, though, 'cause Potus wasn't exactly a puppy anymore and he was out of shape. His tongue hung out and he panted, watching the butterfly make a clean getaway.

"Well, I'm not going to give up as easily as you, Potus. I'm going to keep trying. It's too important to both of us to just quit." There had to be something I could do to get Dad and Miss O'Connor to see eye to eye.

The biggest problem was Gretchen. She was a distraction, for sure. She was beautiful and smart and stylish, but she didn't have that certain something that Team Gravy needed. She didn't make Dad belly-laugh. She thought cosplay was silly. She didn't get his puns, even the ones that were pretty funny. She didn't know how to fix a broken carburetor.

If only Miss O'Connor hadn't gotten sick! They'd been so close! You could practically feel the electricity buzzing between them. If only they had sat down and started to chat. If only they had burned some marshmallows and laughed as they blew out the flames. If only they had looked at each other, really looked at each other! If only, if only, if only . . .

I sighed as Potus lifted his leg on the neighbor's mailbox and then trotted toward our front door. I led him up the front steps, but I stopped at the top and sat down, and the fur monster curled up in a ball at my feet. I patted his head and rubbed his ears and tried to figure out how I was feeling.

Scared. I was feeling scared. What if Dad chose to be with someone who didn't want to be with me? What if he made a new team with someone else?

Dad probably wanted me to pack up my tent and head home—to give up the fight like I'd done when I was five. But I just couldn't. Not this time. I had to give it at least one more try. Miss O'Connor fit with us. She made the whole picture make sense. Dad deserved a beautifully completed puzzle. And so did I.

29

Plotting

I made Bea volunteer to help haul my stuff up to my new room as soon as the carpet was installed. She showed up wearing bib overalls and a bandana covering her hair, like she'd looked up "What to wear when doing chores" in a book. I was wearing a sparkly llama sweatshirt and jeans. I didn't think you needed to dress down to move boxes.

I huffed up the ladder, a box blocking my view of Bea. "It was terrible. Pretty much the worst possible ending to that scenario . . ." I'd promised Bea a sleepover after we were finished dragging boxes up the wobbly ladder. But all I could think about was last week's puke-tastic incident with Miss O'Connor and my dad and the marshmallows that remained untoasted.

"He really likes her. And she likes him. They just need to talk about it." I was slightly out of breath from my mil-lionth trip up to the attic, so I flopped down on the one item Dad had helped with, my bed, which was unmade in one of the window alcoves.

Bea decided it was time for a break too. She pulled a bag of Skittles out of her overnight bag and started to divide them up. I popped a can of Pringles and handed her a Dr Pepper from the mini-fridge.

Bea chose one purple Skittle and chewed it carefully. "I think you're right. When he saw her in the candlelight . . . I mean, before the barf . . . they both had heart eyeballs."

"But now it's like none of it even happened. Miss O'Connor went home, and Dad hung out with Gretchen. The barfing completely broke the spell."

I took a presidential bobblehead doll out of its box and stared into our first president's face. My old room had had a ledge that went all the way around and it had been full of these guys. They would need a new home. I set George Washington's big noggin bobbing before placing him lovingly back in the box.

"They just need to spend more time together. Alone." Bea flipped through the playlist on her iPad until she found a song that she liked and then started to bob her head, not unlike George.

"Yeah, except how am I supposed to get them to do that?"

We chewed in silence for a few minutes. Bea made my

bed for me, tucking the sheets in military-style, while I flipped through a magazine on the floor.

When the next song came on, Bea said, "I got it. They need, like, to get stuck in an elevator. That always works in movies."

"I don't know how to break an elevator," I said. "But otherwise, it's not a bad plan."

"They'd have to talk because they'd be so bored and hungry and mad." Bea tossed one of my throw pillows onto the bed and then straightened it by half a millimeter.

"I'm not sure bored, hungry, and mad are the feelings that help people fall in love. What they need is to be locked on a date. Like the lock-in the youth group just had . . ." My brain started to speed up, flipping through ideas as fast as I could relay them to Bea. "We could lure them to the church basement under false pretenses and then set up a romantic candlelit dinner. With food and music and everything. Therefore, no hunger. So at least we'd be eliminating one of the bad elevator feelings."

Bea frowned. "Luring under false pretenses reminds me of, like . . . abduction."

I stuck my tongue out at her, but I was on a roll. "And we could tie them together! So they'd have to talk!" I added.

"What? No! Now you are seriously describing abduction.

We're not tying anyone together!" she said, shaking her head.

"Fine. Locking them in should do the trick. They'll talk and eat and look into each other's eyes and then . . . magic."

Bea sighed. "It does usually work in the movies. I'll help you with the setup and stuff, but the luring is all on you. That's where I draw the line. I won't be an accomplice in the kidnapping of two adults."

"They'll be so grateful to us once they find each other that it won't even matter," I assured her, shoveling a stack of chips in my mouth.

We decided that the next Wednesday night would be the best time to catch both Dad and Miss O'Connor at church. We cleaned the church basement with the fervor of a criminal cleaning a crime scene, which Bea kept reminding me was basically true.

We set up a romantic date atmosphere. A cluttered closet off the fellowship hall contained decorations from a mishmash of weddings. We found a white linen tablecloth, a few long candles in holders, and a slightly dusty flower arrangement. Bea wanted to be in charge of the music. She picked the soundtrack to a cartoon, but at least it was a cartoon where people fell in love, so I allowed it.

We dimmed the lights, lit the candles, and warmed up a whole pizza we discovered in the refrigerator that the youth group hadn't managed to devour at their last event.

When everything was in place, we stood back and surveyed our hostage situation/date. I had a very good feeling about this. Now to lock them in.

My dad was finishing up some stuff in his office at the church on Wednesday night, so I used the basement phone to call Miss O'Connor. I disguised my voice and said that the church was flooded and that I was looking for volunteers to come clean it up.

"Is she coming?" Bea asked nervously.

"Yeah," I said. "But she sounded annoyed."

"She'll be less annoyed when she sees the basement isn't under water," Bea said.

"Grace, Bea, you guys ready to go?" Dad yelled down the stairs.

"We can't let him see all this"—I gestured around to the date setup—"until Miss O'Connor gets here. He'll know what we're trying to do."

Bea tapped her chin. "Okay, you go stall him. I'll make sure Miss O'Connor doesn't come upstairs. Oh, and get their phones! We don't want anyone calling for backup."

"You're super smart, Bea." I dashed up the stairs.

"You owe me!" she called after me.

"Done studying?" Dad asked. I'd told him that Bea and I needed to come with him to church that afternoon so that we'd have a quiet place to work on our projects. My throat tightened around the lie I was about to tell.

"Almost. There was one thing I needed your help with, though. Can I borrow your phone?"

Dad cocked one eyebrow but handed over his phone. "Sure."

I held up my hand and turned around like I was making a call. Inside, my heart hammered in my chest. What if Miss O'Connor showed up right now? What if Dad went downstairs and saw our setup? What if I couldn't think of anything to say to this fake person I was supposedly talking to on Dad's phone? Sweat broke out on my forehead.

Bea's voice called from the basement, "Um, can you come help with that thing?"

Someone mumbled, "What's going on here?"

I recognized Miss O'Connor's voice. She must have come in from the other side of the building. I grabbed Dad's hand and dragged him down the stairs. "You see, there's this thing we need you to help with."

"Yes, you already mentioned that. What's going on?"

"Um, we think someone left one of the stoves on in the kitchen. And we can't figure out how to turn it off."

I slipped his phone in my pocket. As we landed at the bottom of the stairs, I pushed him through the doors of the fellowship hall, at the same time Bea squeezed out. We pulled the doors closed and twisted the lock, peering at our prisoners through the small rectangular windows.

"What in the devil is going on here?" Dad roared, and Miss O'Connor banged at the doors, pounding with her fists and tugging on the handles.

"Let us out of here right this minute!" she yelled, and swayed on her feet, stumbling over to a chair. "Oh my gosh. Walls closing in. Feeling faint."

Dad's face changed from contorted with rage to full of concern. He sat down in the chair next to her and put a cautious hand on her shoulder. "Are you okay?"

"I don't like being locked in. Get a bit claustrophobic."

Dad looked at us in the windows. "Do you hear that? She's claustrophobic and you've locked her in. Whatever it is you're planning is not going to work, Grace. Let us out."

I looked at Bea and she looked at me. I cleared my throat. "It's a really big room. She should be fine. And we'll let you out in one hour."

"An hour! You've lost your mind. I'm calling . . . hey, my phone!"

I wiggled it in the window, and Bea wiggled Miss O'Connor's. That made Miss O'Connor laugh, and then Dad laughed and their eyeballs glued together for just half a second before they remembered they were prisoners.

Dad lowered his voice and spoke through gritted teeth. "Grace, this is ridiculous. You have to let us out immediately. This is not the way grown-ups do things."

"Yeah, but the way grown-ups do things isn't working, so this is the way kids do things. Eat some pizza. And be nice. We'll be back in an hour."

Bea and I practically skipped out of there, sure we'd made a love connection. Before long they'd be laughing, talking about what an adorable rascal I am, and looking into each other's eyes.

We went upstairs in the empty church and raided the animal crackers in the preschool supply closet. They were slightly stale, but I was so happy with myself I didn't mind.

We played about a million rounds of charades to pass the time. I did an amazing impression of a cuckoo bird, but I always forgot you weren't allowed to make sounds. And since Bea is basically the rules police, I was losing big-time.

I bit the head off a lion cracker. "What do you think they're doing right now?" I asked, crumbs spraying everywhere.

"Thinking up punishments for you," Bea said.

I laughed. "Come on. Dad hasn't punished me for anything in . . . well, since Mom. That's not how Team Gravy operates."

Bea shrugged. "That's how parents operate. He looked royally cheesed off."

"Sure, at first. But after he's had some pizza and he and Miss O'Connor have shared their hopes and dreams, he'll see it was all for his own good."

"I hope you're right because it's time to let them out."

An hour had gone by. Had it been enough time? Would everything be okay now? My knees shook as we walked back down to the fellowship hall. But nothing could prepare me for what we saw when we unlocked the double doors. Miss O'Connor was gone, and Dad looked madder than I'd ever seen him.

"What happened? How did she leave?" I asked. Bea tried to squeeze behind me, like a toddler playing hide-and-seek.

"We were rescued," Dad growled.

Miss Regina emerged from the kitchen, wearing black cropped pants and a leopard-print shirt. She smiled when she saw us, but there was a mean glint in her eye.

"Miss Regina," I said.

"You have quite a lot of explaining to do, young lady. If I hadn't driven by and seen the chair stuffed under the back door, your poor father might've wasted away in here."

"What were you thinking? Why on earth would you do this?" Dad's hands were balled into fists. He looked like a different person, anger twisting up his face.

"I . . . we wanted you and Miss O'Connor to talk." I glanced at Miss Regina, who listened intently. "Like on a date." She burst out laughing but stopped short when I glared at her.

"Sorry, it's just . . ." She leaned over and put a hand on Dad's shoulder. "I just can't see you two together is all."

"Neither can she. She was mad enough to chew through the door. It's a good thing Miss Regina showed up when she did." For a second there was a flicker of confusion and hurt in his eyes.

"So you didn't talk at all? You didn't tell her . . . how you feel or anything? All you did was complain about being locked in without your phones?"

Dad stood up. "I don't want to hear one more word about it. Bea, I'll be giving your mother a call after I drop you off. And, Grace, you're grounded. No leaving the house except school and church. And the rest of your time will be spent doing chores. No computer. And no TV."

He looked frantic to make the punishment sound extra scary, but the truth is, anything he would've dealt me would've stung. Usually, when I flew off the handle and did something *unwise*, we'd talk it out. He'd tell me not to do it again. We'd snap right back to being best friends. But not this time. He was determined to make me feel the bite of the punishment. "And no desserts!" he added.

Tears streamed down my face, and I turned on my heels and smashed right into Bea, bonking our heads together painfully. We walked up the stairs and out to the truck without speaking. *How did things go so terribly wrong?* This was never what happened in the movies when people got locked in elevators. It wasn't even what happened when kids did sneaky stuff to their parents. I was being punished, and Dad was mad, and the whole plan had been a big failure.

I sniffed loudly and wiped snot on the back of my arm. "Well, that didn't quite work out." I opened the truck door and slid in. Bea didn't reply.

I continued. "I mean, I wasn't expecting them to fall in love, but I sure wasn't expecting this garbage fire."

Still nothing from Bea.

"Hey." I touched her knee, but she wouldn't look at me. "Great, now you're mad at me too?"

"Well, now I'm in trouble, and it was mostly your idea! I don't know why I go along with these things."

"Mostly my idea? You're the one who came up with locking them in! Plus, nobody forced you to hide in the closet and eat a million pounds of animal crackers!"

Dad opened the truck door, and we got quiet. He drove us home, dropping Bea in her driveway before parking in ours. She didn't turn and wave when she got to the door. Dad and I walked into our house without saying a word to each other.

I planned to escape to my room, but Dad wasn't done yelling at me.

"I can't believe my daughter *lied* to my friend and told her the church flooded. Of course she rushed over to help. Because that's the kind of person Olivia is. I've never been more disappointed in you, Grace."

Dad was disappointed. In me. He had never said those words before, ever. Heat crept up my neck.

"I'm not sure I can ever look that poor woman in the eye again," Dad said.

"Miss Regina?" I asked hopefully.

"No, *Olivia*!"

My voice wobbled. "Was she super mad?"

Dad rubbed the back of his neck. He needed a shave. His chin was stubbly and his hair was a mess. "She wasn't exactly mad. I mean, once the claustrophobia calmed down. We talked for a few minutes, until Miss Regina showed up to save us. Then she couldn't get out of there fast enough."

I groaned. "Dad, that's because everyone knows Miss Regina has a thing for you. I'm sure Miss O'Connor saw her with her paws all over you and got discouraged again!"

"Enough, Grace. Miss Regina and I are just friends. Olivia and I are just friends. We all attend the same church. Stop trying to make all of this into something it's not. Stay out of my love life. I mean it."

Stay out of my love life. Maybe what he really meant to say was *Stay out of my life.* Dad was lonely, and I'd made things worse instead of better. Some teammate I turned out to be.

30

Picky Piccata

"I just think if you two spend some more time together, you might find you have a lot in common." Dad arranged the magazines on the coffee table as though Gretchen would score him on tidiness after dinner.

"What exactly do we have in common?" I grumped. I had been grounded for exactly three days following the hostage situation, and I was not enjoying my imprisonment. So far it included a lot of extra chores, no TV, and no time with Bea. Which didn't really matter, 'cause as far as I knew she was still mad at me for getting her in trouble. And now, as the cherry on top, I was forced to spend an evening with Dad and Gretchen. The urge to sabotage was strong.

I realized that Dad still hadn't answered my question, so I stared hard at him until he said, "I don't know! That's why you need to spend time together! There must be something."

I sighed. "Fine."

"After dinner, Gretchen suggested we all sit down and watch a movie together. She mentioned *Country Bridges*. Have you seen that one?"

"Uh, isn't that the one with all the old people kissing?" I asked, plopping down on the couch.

Dad was defensive. "It won all kind of awards. And . . . I'm sure other stuff happens besides the kissing."

"Ew. Not exactly the type of movie you want to watch with your dad and his girlfriend," I mumbled.

Dad started flipping through our DVDs. "Maybe there's something else in here that we might all enjoy. Do you think she's seen *America's Bloodiest Battles*?"

"I'm guessing no. Good luck convincing her to check it out," I said.

"Hey, you wanted less kissing."

"So, what are we ordering for dinner?" I asked. My mouth watered at the thought of pizza.

Dad straightened up with a handful of DVDs in his arms. "We are going to cook dinner for Gretchen."

"Say what," I said, staring at my dad like he'd grown a second head.

"You and I are going to prepare a nice meal for Gretchen. Together. Using all of our combined cooking skills. And YouTube. We will definitely need to consult YouTube. But I think it's time we learned to be more self-sufficient."

I snorted. "You just want to show off for Gretchen."

"If Gretchen is impressed with our culinary skills, so be it. Now come in here and help me."

The recipe we were attempting was for chicken piccata and angel-hair pasta. Dad also ambitiously thought we should have some kind of garlic bread and salad with it. The printed recipe was spread out on the counter, right next to the grocery bags. He'd gone shopping earlier, and as he read through the recipe, I was surprised to find he had managed to get everything we needed.

We alternated between Dad reading a step of the recipe and me Googling how to actually do that step, and slowly but surely, the meal came together. The kitchen was a mess, and there were dirty dishes piled on pretty much every surface. But an hour later we had cooked chicken, delicious sauce, al dente pasta, toasted garlic bread, and salad all sitting on the kitchen table, just as the doorbell rang.

Dad greeted Gretchen with a hug. She took off her expensive-looking coat and smoothed her dress. She had a fresh manicure and just the right amount of makeup and of course looked perfect, but her smile was tight and it didn't quite make it up to her eyes.

"Grace, how nice that you'll be spending the evening with us," she said. "Your dad tells me you've been sticking close to home lately." She cocked an eyebrow at me and I just smiled like a wooden puppet.

"I hope you're hungry, 'cause Grace and I whipped up a delicious Italian feast for you!" Dad said, leading her to the kitchen.

Gretchen surveyed the table and patted Dad on the arm. "Well done. And I see you didn't even burn the kitchen down."

Dad's face got serious. "Did you hear about the Italian chef who died?" He paused for dramatic effect. "He pasta way."

Dad and I cracked up, but Gretchen only half smiled.

"His legacy will become a pizza history!" I said, giving Gretchen the same look my dad always gives me after a punny joke.

"Clever," she said, sitting down. "I'm sorry, I should have told you that I just started cutting carbs this week. No pasta or bread for me."

Dad's face fell, but only a tiny fraction. "That's perfectly fine. You can still have chicken and salad."

"No sauce, though. That looks rich," she said, sipping daintily from her water.

Dad shrugged, and we all filled our plates. I ate extra pasta and garlic bread to make up for Gretchen's diet. It was delicious. And that sauce! I couldn't believe that me and Dad had pulled that off! It was a form of gravy, I guess, so that made sense.

Gretchen turned to me. "Grace, tell me about your plans for the summer?"

"Oh, well, Dad and I are planning a bunch of little road trips to try and visit all these wacky presidential sites. And then we were hired to portray Teddy and Alice at the World's Fare in July—you know about that already."

I was pretty much daring her to say something bad about me and Dad and the stuff we like to do. But she went another direction with it.

"When I was your age, I loved to go to summer camp. For the entire summer. It was so much fun, making new friends and spending time in nature."

Dad looked down at his plate and I swallowed my last bit of chicken. "That's . . . nice," I said cautiously.

"Maybe you and your dad should look into some camps? That might be more fun for you, and less driving and dress-up for him!"

I jerked my head toward Dad, who just shrugged and gave me the *What do you think?* look.

"Um, no. Me and Dad like all the extra time we get to spend together during the summer. We already have plans."

"Maybe next year, then," Gretchen said, taking a slow sip of her water.

After dinner, Gretchen suggested I clean up the kitchen and clear the table so she and Dad could get the movie ready. Normally, I would've been irritated that she was ordering me around, but if cleaning the kitchen meant I didn't have to endure any more not-so-subtle hints to get lost, I was a happy volunteer.

I carried the dishes to the sink and filled it with warm soapy water. We had a dishwasher, but tonight felt like a good time to do things the old-fashioned way.

Is this what my life would be if Dad got married? Would I spend all my time staying out of the way and hoping Mommy Dearest wouldn't talk to me?

Not if the lady was Miss O'Connor.

Dad's phone was abandoned on the table and I picked it up and considered calling her. There was something I wanted to tell her. I'd followed up on her Edith Roosevelt comment at the Muffins with Mom event and done some extra research on the early years of the Roosevelt family.

It turned out that Teddy Roosevelt had sent his baby daughter to live with an aunt after his first wife died. He was so heartbroken he couldn't even bear to look at little Alice. And it was only after he'd been married again, to Edith, that she insisted Alice come home. Edith had given

Alice her father back instead of taking him away. And by loving him, she'd helped to heal his heart and make him a better father to Alice. She had stitched the broken family back together again, even if it looked a bit different and was frayed around the edges.

That's what I wanted to tell Miss O'Connor, plus so much more, but my finger froze over the Call button.

Dad stuck his head in the kitchen. "You done yet? We want to get this movie going."

I dropped Dad's phone and stuck my guilty hands back in the bubbles. "A few more dishes here. I'll be done in a second."

"Okay," Dad said, and returned to his guest.

I dried the last dish and put it in the cabinet, and then used a wet cloth to wipe down the table. When there wasn't anything else I could reasonably clean in the kitchen, I trudged into the living room.

And stopped dead in my tracks.

And wished my eyeballs could fall out of my eyes.

Gretchen was kissing my dad.

On the mouth.

"It looks like you guys need to be alone!" I snarled, and spun on my heels through the kitchen and out the back door.

31

Joy-less Ride

My head spun and I was far from thinking clearly.

My dad.

Was kissing.

Her.

The woman who laughs at none of his jokes and wants to send me away for the entire summer.

Kissing. In my living room. Where I live.

I ran, my feet pounding the sidewalk, my heart beating in my ears. The same words repeated in my head over and over. *Team Gravy. Team Gravy. Team Gravy.*

My arms worked double-time, and tears streaked my face. A car horn blared as I crossed an intersection without so much as a glance across the street.

I wanted my dad to be happy. I wanted him to go on dates and meet the right person so he wouldn't be lonely anymore.

But Gretchen? She isn't the right fit. She isn't the right piece.

When my feet finally stopped running, I stood outside the First Baptist Church. My second home, until a few busybodies had started putting ideas in my dad's head. I bent and picked a marble-sized rock out of the landscaping and flung it at the double doors of the church.

Dad kissing Gretchen.

Chunk.

Kissing her!

Chunk.

She makes him drink soy lattes!

Chunk.

And watch boring movies.

Chunk.

She doesn't get us.

Chunk.

Again and again I threw rocks until my arms hurt, but the door didn't even have the tiniest scratch on it. I bent down in search of a larger rock and saw my salvation out of the corner of my eye.

The church van.

It was parked in the covered drop-off area.

Shiny and white and completely forbidden for anyone to borrow unless they had express written permission from a whole slew of committees.

Including the Building and Grounds Committee.

Don't mind if I do.

I marched over and pressed my nose to the driver's-side window.

The keys swung from the ignition.

My heart hammered in my ears, and I felt my fingertips go tingly as I gripped the door handle. *I'm only twelve! I know how to drive in theory. . . .* All my skills came from the video games at the pizza parlor. I'd be in so much trouble from the church. From my dad. And somehow the thought thrilled me.

I remembered that disgusting kiss again, and before I knew it, I'd opened the door and climbed into the driver's seat. I quickly buckled my seat belt, because I could hear Bea's voice in my head, telling me that if I was going to be reckless, I should at least be safety-conscious. And like a slam in the guts, I remembered that Bea wasn't actually speaking to me at the moment. One twist of the keys and the engine purred.

As I popped the gearshift into drive, the bald-headed van driver came out the church doors. His eyes widened when he saw me, but I gunned it before he had a chance to grab the passenger door. I flew out of the parking lot, my knuckles white on the steering wheel and my feet barely reaching the pedals.

At first it was exhilarating. *I'm driving! Like a grown-up!*

On the roads and everything! It wasn't as hard as I thought. You stopped at stop signs. You steered in a mostly straight line. You tried to avoid other cars and people and dogs and bicycles and stuff. *Easy-peasy.* Somehow that didn't make me feel any more relaxed, though.

What in the world was I doing? Where would I go? Had I actually stolen the church van? I started to laugh, not because any of it was funny, but because I had so much pent-up energy, excitement, anger, I wasn't sure what, and it just spilled out in manic giggles.

"I am so dead." I laughed as I turned down a gravel road headed out of town. Better to be off the main square, away from as many people as possible. A green highway sign loomed ahead, and I slammed on my brakes with a little too much force to read it.

Springfield 30 Miles
Branson 74 Miles
St. Louis 236 Miles

My mind flashed to the billiken statue that looked like President Taft. One of our unpinned destinations on the presidential bucket list that would probably never get done now that Dad was with Gretchen the history hater. My foot hit the gas and I sped up, bouncing over a bump that made my teeth clank together.

I had a plan. I was going to St. Louis to rub a billiken belly. In a stolen van. That I didn't technically know how to drive. *What could go wrong?*

I found out ten short minutes later.

A deer jumped out from a clump of trees lining the road. I didn't even have time to hit the brakes. I screamed, my hands flew to cover my face, and the crash and thud told me the van would be coming to a complete and total stop. When I stopped shaking enough to pull the door handle, I tumbled out, my legs almost buckling beneath me.

What have I done?

I am so, so dead.

And so is this deer, apparently.

I started to cry, kneeling there in the gravel next to the bloody deer.

I needed help and for the first time in the last three years, the person I wanted was not my dad. Who? Who could I call, when I'd done something so, so bad? Who would know what to say, what to do?

Only one name came to mind.

I stumbled back to the car and opened the glove box. The church's old fat cell phone lay on top of the van's registration, just where I knew it would be. I typed in her number but started to sob before she picked up.

"Hello?"

"Miss O'Connor?"

"Grace, honey, is that you?"

I just cried harder, snot running down my face.

"Where are you? Your dad called me scared as anything. The whole town is out looking for you. I've been driving all over the place. . . ."

"I . . . had an accident." I hoped if I focused on my near escape from physical harm, I might get in less trouble.

"What kind of accident? Where are you? Are you hurt?"

I told her the road I was on, and the last thing I remembered passing. I didn't mention I'd stolen a van or driven illegally before killing an innocent deer. There'd be plenty of time for that later.

"I'm on my way. Don't move one single muscle until I get there, do you hear me?" She sounded so worried about me. Even though I knew I would get the worst punishment of my entire life, it somehow made me feel a smidge better to know that someone as nice as Miss O'Connor cared about me. And my dad, she'd seemed worried about him, too.

And it was while I was sitting there, in the middle of the empty gravel road, that my feelings about Miss O'Connor were confirmed. I loved her.

Miss O'Connor, my history teacher.

Miss O'Connor, who wore weird clothes kinda like me.

Miss O'Connor, who watched documentaries and laughed

at all my dad's jokes, even the sermon ones, which weren't remotely funny.

My ears filled with the sound of whooshing, and my head felt light.

I love Miss O'Connor.

And then I remembered how pink my dad's cheeks got when he talked about their night at the bonfire.

Sharing his books with her.

Smiling and rolling his eyes at her wacky outfits.

Maybe he loves her, too.

We needed her to stitch us back together, like Edith stitched up Teddy and Alice. I let out a breath as her little blue VW Bug came into view and wondered how I could untangle this giant mess I'd made.

Miss O'Connor jumped out of her car and ran to kneel beside me on the road. "Grace, are you hurt? What happened?" she asked, pushing my hair back from my face. I stared at her like I was maybe seeing her for the first time. She was here. She had come. I had needed her and she had rescued me. Her voice seemed almost frantic as she helped me stand and led me to her car. "Do you have any idea how dangerous this was? Not to mention completely illegal. What if you'd been stopped by the police?"

My head nodded so fast I started to feel nauseous. Or maybe my body was coming down from the thrill of driving. And I wasn't sure if my headache was from Miss O'Connor's lecture, or the cracking impact of the van with the deer, which was still snuggling the asphalt.

"You could've been arrested! You still might if the church decides to press charges."

Arrested? I didn't even think about that. I'd only been focused on making the Building and Grounds Committee mad and making my dad pay for what he'd done. My hands and then my knees began to shake. Miss O'Connor paused her lecture to pop the trunk of her blue Bug. She pulled out a soft plaid blanket and wrapped it around my shoulders.

"Come sit in my car," she said, her voice a few degrees warmer.

Once we were sitting in the bucket seats, she twisted to face me. "Can you please just tell me what happened? What made you think grand theft auto was a good idea?"

I let out a slow breath. "My dad . . . We had Gretchen over for dinner."

Miss O'Connor's face hid any kind of reaction. "Go on" was all she said.

"So, she told me to clean up the kitchen and wash the dishes and then I walked into the living room. . . ."

It began to rain. Fat drops plopped down the curved windshield of the Bug. I wondered if the deer would be cold, but then I remembered it was dead, so it wouldn't.

"Grace?"

"They kissed! It was terrible and disgusting and I wanted to scoop my own eyeballs out with a spoon! And I don't want it to be her. I want it to be you."

"Wait, what? Slow down. This is a lot of information."

So I took a deep breath and I told her everything again, but more slowly. I paused after the kissing part to really let it sink in. Miss O'Connor looked seasick, which is exactly how I felt about the whole thing.

"I was so mad, at Dad and at the bossy ladies at church and at Gretchen. . . . I saw the van sitting there, and it seemed like the perfect way to get back at everyone."

Miss O'Connor nodded. "Except you don't know how to drive."

"Except that. And except this deer doesn't know how to look both ways before crossing the street."

We both smiled sadly.

Miss O'Connor reached over and rubbed my blanket-covered shoulder. "Oh, Grace, you were so lucky! You could've been killed, do you know that?"

I shrugged, and Miss O'Connor took a deep breath, watching the rain come down.

"I called your dad. He's on his way."

I felt my heart drop to my feet. So this is it. The End. I'm probably going to be sent off to boarding school or something and Dad will marry that horrible woman, and my life will be over. And Team Gravy will definitely be over.

"What you said . . . about wanting it to be me . . . I know you *think* that's how your dad feels—"

"It is. He likes you. You're the only person who . . . fits with us. Who gets us. Who's there for us. He knows that. But he thinks you don't feel the same way about him."

"And I thought he didn't feel that way about me," she said softly.

"That's why I've tried to push you two together. You both need to tell each other how you feel, so we can be a family."

Miss O'Connor laughed and shook her head. "It's not always so simple, Grace."

"Grown-ups make things too complicated sometimes."

She didn't respond because just then something banged on the passenger-side window. My dad dripped in the rain, his face as furious as I'd ever seen it. It was time to look my dad in the eye and swallow the punishment for all the stuff I'd done. I gave Miss O'Connor's hand one more squeeze before stepping out of the car into the rain.

32

Come Clean

Dad was silent the entire way home, but his hands shook on the truck's steering wheel. A few times he opened his mouth to say something but then snapped it shut again.

When we got to our house, I trudged up to my room and lay on my bed. The space smelled like new paint and fresh carpet. Dad had helped me hang goofy posters on the walls and I'd spent hours arranging all my new bookshelves. The whole room was just a huge reminder of all the possibilities between Dad and me that were done now.

"Knock knock," Dad said, sticking his head up through the floor opening. "Can I come in?"

I sighed. I couldn't avoid this talk forever. "Yes." I made room for him on the bed without risking eye contact. He plopped down but didn't say anything, and as the seconds ticked by, my need to confess grew.

"Since I'm already in the most trouble I will ever be in

in my whole entire life, I feel like I need to tell you something."

"There's more?" Dad asked, turning to face me. "How is that possible?"

I let out a long breath and stared at the ceiling. "Well . . . when Miss Donna and Miss Marge first suggested you start dating, I thought you were just going along with it to make them happy. I didn't realize that you were . . . that you were lonely. So I was angry. And I sabotaged a few of your dates."

I turned to look at him. My dad's features flicked through just about every known emotion and landed on confused.

"You messed up my dates?"

I nodded and took a deep breath. "I may have also tampered with your Lid for Every Pot account. Clarissa Washington was me. And I stole your wallet and there was the incident with the chicken and the fart picnic. . . ." I said the whole thing in one long gasp and then closed my eyes and braced for the worst.

Dad's voice was high-pitched and a little panicky. "Clarissa was you. . . . Also, I *knew* you masterminded the fart picnic!"

I snuck a peek at him. He seemed like he was swallowing a lot more than a normal person. Finally, he spoke.

"Why would you do that?"

Stinging tears filled my eyes again. "Because I thought that if you started dating and eventually got married you and I wouldn't spend any time together anymore. That we wouldn't be Team Gravy anymore."

Dad's face softened, and he leaned over and wiped a tear off my cheek. "Oh, Grace. That could never happen. Even if I did fall in love and get married, you would always be my number one girl. You and me . . . this isn't going anywhere. No matter what."

"But you told me to stay out of your love life. And right now, that's your whole entire life!"

"I was angry when I said that. I meant you should stop locking people in basements. I never meant you should stay out of my life completely. You *are* my life, Grace."

"I love you, Dad," I said in a squeaky voice.

"Oh, honey, I love you, too. So so much. I . . . ended things with Gretchen. When I went to chase after you, she told me to let you go."

I gulped. "So it was my fault you guys broke up." Even though that's what I'd wanted, it felt worse than I'd imagined. I didn't want my dad to be sad. I wanted the opposite of that. I felt guilt squirm in my guts like soggy spaghetti.

"Giblet, look at me." He cupped my chin so I looked into his face. "It was not your fault that things went wrong between me and Gretchen. You were right about her from the beginning. She wasn't the best fit for us."

I pictured that darn White House puzzle with one piece missing.

Dad flopped back on my bed with his arms behind his head, and I did the same thing. We stared at my freshly painted ceiling for a quiet moment, each of us lost in our own thoughts.

"You said you *were* sabotaging my dates. What made you stop?" he asked after a while.

I remembered that single tear running down Dad's cheek on lasagna disaster night. "I wanted you to find the right person."

"And you think the right person is Olivia," he concluded.

"I think you know," I said softly. "If this team ever took on a third person, I would want it to be her. It's gotta be her."

"When you were gone . . . when we couldn't find you anywhere . . ." Dad's Adam's apple bobbed and his eyes flicked all over my room. "Olivia was the first person I thought of to call."

"That's because she is the ONE, Dad!" I said, reaching over to squeeze his hand.

"Well . . . maybe it's time I got brave, then. I can take a risk. I would do just about anything for you, Grace."

"Don't just do it for me, Dad. Be brave because it's what you want and who you are."

He nodded. "I might need your help, though." He chuckled. "Getting Olivia to fall for me could be our next

Team Gravy project. That is, if you still want to be on a team with me?"

The noodle feeling in my guts melted and for the first time in a long while I felt light, like maybe I had springs in my shoes. I think the feeling was hope. "Let's work together!" I nodded. "Miss O'Connor is about to be smothered with a whole pan of Team Gravy. She won't even know what hit her."

I cornered Bea the next Monday in the hallway at school. "Hey," I said.

"Hey," she said, but she didn't stop walking.

"Hold up for a second," I said.

"I'm still grounded. My mom said she was very disappointed in me when she got that call from your dad!" Bea's glare could have cut glass.

"I am so sorry about that. You were right. It was my idea, and I am always getting you into trouble."

Bea sniffed. "You do come up with some doozies."

"And you're always there to try and make me see reason! Imagine if I'd actually tried to tie my dad and Miss O'Connor together like I suggested!"

Bea laughed. "Yeah, that would have been worse."

"I make you do exciting and scary things, and you make

me think things through and use my head. We make an excellent team," I said.

Bea's mouth screwed into a stifled grin. "Too bad you didn't have my voice of reason to talk you out of stealing the church van . . ."

I groaned. "You heard about that, huh?"

She laughed. "I'm pretty sure the entire town heard about that."

"Well, if it makes you feel better about your measly one-week punishment, I'm grounded until the summer."

Bea smiled. "That does actually make me feel a little bit better."

I chuckled and threw my arm around her shoulder. "I'm glad you and me are gonna be all right. I missed you."

"I missed you, too, but let's stay out of your dad's love life for a while."

"Oh, don't worry. Dad has seen the value in my scheming and he has recruited me to help get him and Miss O'Connor together." I waggled my eyebrows. "She came over after the whole van-stealing night and they talked and talked and by the end of the night the backyard fire pit was going and the s'mores fixings were gone."

"Well then, I guess it was a good thing you and I messed up all of his dates." Bea grinned.

"Of course it was. One of my better ideas, if I do say so myself."

33

Scones and Shrimps

The following Wednesday, I sat through the entire school day like I had fire ants in my pants. Team Gravy had a big surprise planned, and Miss O'Connor had no idea it was coming.

History class, my last of the day, was especially excruciating. The clock barely moved. Miss O'Connor was teaching us all about the Cold War, and I couldn't concentrate at all. I just kept thinking about when the last bell would ring and Dad and I could put our plan into action.

Dad had asked me about a billion times if I was sure I wanted to do this. At school. Where other classmates and teachers might see. This was, after all, a potentially embarrassing thing that we were about to do. I had told him I wasn't afraid of being embarrassed, that I just wanted him to be happy. And I wanted me to be happy. And I wanted Miss O'Connor to be happy.

The last bell rang, and most of the kids scampered out of the classroom like their hair was on fire. Me and Bea stayed behind, slowly packing up our stuff, until we were the last three people in the room. Us and Miss O'Connor.

And then my dad appeared in the doorway, wearing his Abraham Lincoln stovepipe hat. He'd wanted to wear the fake beard, too, but I'd vetoed that. He had a picnic basket slung over one arm and a book tucked into the other.

He cleared his throat. Miss O'Connor looked up, and her hand flew to her mouth. Her eyes were all sparkly. She was giggling, but not in a mean way. Bea and I exchanged a happy look.

"Four score and a bunch of years ago . . . ," Dad began. He tugged at his bow tie. ". . . Grace and I made a wonderful friendship with Miss Olivia O'Connor. Founded on our love for history, bad puns, and *Jungle Survivor*, and dedicated to the proposition that . . ."

I nudged Bea in the ribs. "Here comes the good part."

". . . friendship can grow into something more."

Miss O'Connor seemed frozen. Her hand still covered her mouth, but she wasn't giggling anymore. As Dad's words sank in, he and Miss O'Connor shared a serious eye lock.

"Dad, show her the basket," I whispered. Dad set the wicker basket on her desk and opened the lid. We'd spent the previous afternoon baking some delicious chocolate chip scones. I'd snuck one, and they were scrumptious, if I do say so myself.

"This is a little something Grace and I whipped up. A gift for our favorite lady."

"Miss O'Connor, what my dad is trying to say, is that we made all this for you, to ask if you might go on a date. With my dad. Next weekend, the Springfield Museum is having this special fundraiser. It's black tie, very fancy."

"Just like these scones Grace and I made *all by ourselves*," Dad added.

"It's called the Presidential Portrait Walk. You two can get all dressed up and walk through the paintings and impress each other with the vast amount of history you know. Plus, there will probably be crab cakes and little shrimps on skewers."

"Shrimps . . . ," Miss O'Connor repeated. Possibly still in shock. It's not every day that Abraham Lincoln comes to your classroom and asks you out.

"Give her the book, Dad." He thrust the dusty book into Miss O'Connor's hands and she touched the cover softly, like she was stroking a bird. "*Presidential Portraits Through the Years*," she said, reading the title.

"That's so you can study up before we go. If you want to go, that is. Did you want to go?"

"This is just . . . amazing," she sighed, looking from the book to the basket to Dad and back again. "I've been waiting for this for a very long time."

She might have meant the Presidential Portrait Walk, but I didn't think so.

The next Saturday, I helped Dad get his bow tie just right. He gelled his hair and had a bouquet of flowers waiting by the door.

"This is it, Dad. Your first and hopefully not your last date with Miss O'Connor. Olivia. I should probably start calling her Olivia now. . . . Don't screw it up."

Dad grinned at me. "It will be a lot easier to not screw up if you aren't sabotaging me. You are a criminal mastermind."

I shrugged. "Necessary evil. All my meddling got us where we are today."

The doorbell rang, and I rushed to answer it. Olivia stood on the front step, looking about as beautiful as an angel. She wore a sparkly gold dress, and her wild curls were pulled back in a jeweled clip. She looked at Dad and grinned.

I turned to Dad. "All right, now don't forget what I

told you: If you're going to sneak shrimps home in your pockets, use a plastic sandwich bag."

Olivia pulled one out of her purse and waggled her eyebrows at me. "Why do you think I brought a purse?"

"My kind of lady. You would do well on *Jungle Survivor*, you know that?" Dad said, grinning.

He gave her the flowers and she gave him a hug and as the two of them headed out the door, Dad turned and looked at me.

"You'll be okay here tonight, Giblet?" he asked.

"Dad, go. I'll be just fine."

34

Strong as a Bull Moose

It was the first day of May, and I had chosen a hot-pink dress with colorful pom-poms all over it and a bright green belt. I wanted to feel extra confident because today I was presenting my famous-American project in Miss O'Connor's class.

As soon as the seventh-hour bell rang, Miss O'Connor gave a moving speech about how hard we'd worked and all the growth she had seen in our research notes. She smiled, making all of her students feel special and seen and happy, and I wondered why it had taken me so long to see how beautiful she was.

Bea was super prepared. She had read me her entire presentation the night before. She had made sure she went to bed early and had made herself a power smoothie for breakfast. Her notes were stacked neatly on her desk with her hands folded calmly on top of them.

I, on the other hand, had only practiced my speech once,

and that was to Potus. I had done the research, and I felt like I knew Teddy and Alice back and forth and sideways. But getting up there, in front of my whole class and my dad's new girlfriend (eek!), made my mouth go dry.

My heart hammered in my chest as Miss O'Connor got set up at the back of the room with her timer and her rubric. As long as she didn't call on me first, I would be fine. She should call on Bea. Bea was ready. She was practically vibrating with readiness. As long as I wasn't the very first one—

"Okay, I'm going to go ahead and draw a name for our first victim—Oh, I mean presenter." Miss O'Connor chuckled. "Anyway, the first presentation is . . . Grace Martin." She beamed at me, as if she'd just given me a huge piece of cake.

I clutched my chest as if I was afraid my heart might bust right out of there. Everyone turned to look at me. I gulped. Bea leaned across the aisle. "You got this, Grace. Talking about Teddy is one million times easier than setting your dad up with Miss O'Connor, and you managed to do that."

I stood and walked to the front, clutching my laptop. My fingers shook as I projected my slideshow up on the screen. But when I pushed Play and "Hail to the Chief" started to play, my classmates broke into applause.

"Thank you, everyone. Today, I am going to tell you

why Teddy Roosevelt was our greatest president and a truly inspiring American." I glanced at the screen behind me and gave the picture of Teddy a wink.

"Teddy Roosevelt didn't have the easiest life." I started to flip through the pictures. "He was a sickly child, and he spent a lot of time in bed. He was bullied for his size and because he wore glasses. He lost his mother, and his first wife." The room full of sixth graders went very quiet, like they were holding their breath. My throat tightened, but I pushed thoughts of my own mother out of my head.

"But Teddy was able to do something that was truly amazing. He was able to take these terrible changes in his life and turn them into something good. He didn't just survive. He thrived. He went on to become our twenty-sixth president. He remarried after his first wife died and had five more children. He won a Nobel Peace Prize and went on a dangerous and exciting river expedition. He was pretty much the poster child for taking lemons and making lemonade."

I clicked to the photo of Teddy riding on the back of a moose down a river, and my audience gasped and chuckled. "Teddy Roosevelt is quoted as saying, 'The only man who never makes mistakes is the man who never does anything.' I am trying to learn that changes, new experiences, and even mistakes are all part of life. And if I can be strong, and brave, and embrace the changes, I might someday be as cool as Teddy Roosevelt riding a moose."

My classmates burst into applause, and I caught Bea's eye. She beamed at me and gave me a wink and then rattled the bag of Skittles she had poking out of her backpack pocket. The rest of the presentation went by in a blur. I threw around names, dates, accomplishments, and facts. I told my classmates everything I'd learned about President Roosevelt, and of course his most spirited daughter, Alice.

Miss O'Connor grinned and scribbled a last note on my rubric. "Does anyone have any questions for Grace?" Hands flew up all over the room, and I answered every single one. I especially loved the questions about Alice and Edith and the children. I felt like I was talking about friends, people I'd spent a lot of time with. People I knew by heart.

When the last question was answered and it was time to return to my seat, I flipped to the very last picture in my slideshow. It was of the entire Roosevelt family, sitting happily on the grass. Teddy's hand was on Alice's shoulder and Edith smiled in a gentle, content way. They looked like they belonged together.

I spent the rest of class in a kind of daze. I know that Bea nailed her presentation on Jackie Robinson. I know that a few other kids presented. But mostly my head was in the clouds. Or more accurately, it was in the past, with Teddy and Alice.

After class, Miss O'Connor stopped me as I headed out the door. "Fantastic presentation, Grace. You did the whole Roosevelt family proud."

🍓

There's this feeling you get on a spring Sunday morning, when you step out onto the sidewalk after church and you have the whole day in front of you. I squinted in the sunlight and took a deep breath. The air smelled like fresh-cut grass and warm sunshine. People flowed around me, patting each other on the back and shaking hands. Everyone was smiling.

I closed my eyes, my face tilted toward the sun. I could hear Bea's guitar, the sweet notes of her final song still ringing out as the patrons left the church.

Olivia came and stood next to me in the sunshine. "Great sermon today," she said. "It has me thinking about that person at school who keeps stealing my snacks from the faculty fridge, even when they're so clearly marked."

"Forgiveness is key," I said, quoting my dad's sermon.

"I suppose he's right. Him and God. God's usually right about these things."

Dad emerged from the church but was delayed in joining me and Olivia by the throng of people who wanted to wish him well and compliment him on his sermon and ask for prayers. I didn't mind, though. I was just about as happy as I could be standing in the sunshine with Olivia, listening to Bea, waiting for Dad.

Bea's parents stood under the shade of a large oak tree, Mrs. Morrison bouncing Julian on her hip. The old ladies of the congregation were taking turns cooing over Bea's little brother, straightening his tiny bow tie and tickling his chubby knees. His parents beamed, and I wasn't even mad at them for being so happy. They had rearranged their family, but it had all turned out okay. Maybe even better than okay.

Dad finally escaped his crowd of adoring fans and he kissed the top of my head and put his arm around Olivia's shoulders. "Hey! There you are. How would you two like to join me for lunch at Ziggy's? I'm in the mood for a three-meat combo."

I was just about to give my enthusiastic reply when I overheard a woman's voice from behind me on the steps.

"Pastor Davy is dating Olivia O'Connor! Well, I suppose she is a nice young lady. We did say he should find a nice young lady. But what's taking him so long? Why doesn't he pop the question? They aren't getting any younger. As members of the Building and Grounds Committee, I really feel we should let him know that he'd better ask for her hand."

I felt my ears go red, and my hands balled into fists. The voice clearly belonged to Miss Donna, and when I spun on my heels to confront her, I saw that she was talking to Miss Marge. So predictable.

"Miss Donna, Miss Marge, with all due respect . . . ," I started, my voice quaking with rage, "mind your own beeswax!"

"Grace!" Dad said, his eyes bugging. Olivia grabbed his arm, looking between me and him and the church busy-bodies.

I took a few deep breaths and tried to find Bea's guitar notes over the chatter of the people on the steps. The church bells started to chime, giving me a few more seconds to calm down, to think of Team Gravy and Olivia and what would be best for everyone.

When the last note of the last bell died down I straightened my spine and pushed back my shoulders. I looked those two women right in the face. "My dad has taken your advice and found a nice lady to spend time with. Now, if it's okay with the two of you, I think we might want to stay out of it for a while so they can figure things out."

Miss Donna sniffed. "I love a spring proposal."

Miss Marge nodded. "I love a summer wedding."

Dad held up both hands in surrender. "Ladies! I'm with Grace on this one. Let's not get ahead of ourselves." He turned to look at Olivia. "I have somehow managed to convince the most awesome woman in the entire congregation to go out with me. Let's not scare her off."

Miss Marge leaned her white puffball hair toward Dad and spoke in the world's loudest whisper. "You'd better lock that down before she figures out you tell those terrible jokes all the time."

Dad busted out laughing, which was totally contagious, and so me and Olivia joined in. "Oh no," Dad snorted, "my secret's out!"

When he'd wiped the tears from his eyes, he turned to Miss Marge and Miss Donna. "Ladies. Thank you for looking out for me. For wanting what's best for me. But I gotta make my own decision on this one. Don't worry. I'm talking to the Big Guy about it. So how 'bout we wait until He tells me what to do?"

The ladies smiled and nodded and looked slightly abashed, because even if you can argue with a pastor, you can't argue with God. I slipped one arm through my dad's and one through Olivia's and smiled, because I was pretty sure Olivia was the answer to the preacher's prayers.

35

Finishing Touch

"Today is a very special day in the history of Team Gravy," I said, looking Dad and Olivia in the eye. "A day we have been anticipating for quite some time. A day that will dramatically change our lives."

Dad snorted. I ignored him.

"Today, we tour my new, awesome, and completely unpacked bedroom. Follow me," I said, heading up the stairs with Olivia and Dad trailing behind.

I stopped at the top of the stairs and admired the space that was now all mine. Just a few short months ago it had been stuffed to the ceiling with boxes of junk. The cobwebs and dust had made it seem more haunted than not. Plus, there had been a definite lack of walls, ceiling, heating, and cooling. You know, the basics.

But now, looking around, it was like this room had been designed just for me. The slanting ceilings and walls had been painted a soft yellow that felt like pure sunshine. There was a cool, modern chandelier hanging in the center of the space that reminded me of a lacy beach ball. The soft, squishy carpet still gave off that new smell, and a colorful area rug added some personality.

My sewing machine sat on an L-shaped table in one of the window alcoves. The space to spread out in the natural light had spurred me to sew all the curtains and pillows with bright funky fabrics. The dress form I'd found at a garage sale sat waiting for me to make it a costume. I thought I might be Dolley Madison for Halloween.

My bed was set up in the other window alcove. The crisp white bedspread was the perfect background to show off my colorful pillows. I could see the stars when I lay there at night. Low shelves lined one wall, filled with a rainbow of book spines.

Olivia let out a whistle. "Bravo! You guys did an amazing job up here!" She walked around, inspecting little details. Dad proudly explained how we ran the heating ducts and installed the pink insulation. "My assistant, Grace, should get a lot of the credit here. She hammers like lightning."

"'Cause I'm so fast?" I asked.

"'Cause lightning never strikes the same place twice, is more like it." Dad cracked up, and I stuck my tongue out at him.

Our wacky presidential bucket list map was proudly

hung on the wall, with all the colorful pins marking the places we've already been. I couldn't wait to add some more over the summer, once I was no longer grounded and I could start leaving the house again.

"There's a familiar face," Olivia said, pointing to the poster of Teddy Roosevelt.

"He's practically part of the family," I said, winking at my dad.

Olivia spied the last lonely cardboard box sitting in the corner. "What's this?" she asked, nudging the box with her toe.

"My presidential bobbleheads. I have a ton of them, and I'm not really sure where to put them. I thought about on top of the bookshelves, but I want them to have their own kind of space."

Olivia tapped her chin thoughtfully. "Your dad mentioned that. I think I might have the perfect thing. That is, if you like quirky, eclectic style?" She lifted one eyebrow.

Dad jumped in. "Have you met Grace? Olivia, may I introduce you to my very quirky, very eclectic daughter, Grace Martin."

I curtsied, lifting the hem of my rainbow-printed skirt, and Olivia giggled. "Fair point. It's out in the truck, maybe Davy can help me carry it in?"

I shrugged, but my curiosity was piqued. "Sounds interesting." While Dad and Olivia hauled whatever it was out of Dad's truck, I turned on some music and threw a ball for Potus.

I could hear them shuffling below the trapdoor long before I could see them. "You go through first, and I'll pass it up to you," Dad's disembodied voice said. Olivia popped through the door, smiled at me, and yelled, "All right, give it a shove!" This was giving me major flashbacks from the day we tried to push the Christmas tree box up here.

Dad grunted and an object that looked strangely like an old-fashioned car burst through the floor. Olivia helped Dad guide it, and then he came through after, panting.

"Whew. They don't make 'em like that anymore. That thing weighs about a million pounds."

Olivia collapsed on the floor next to Dad. "I hope she likes it, 'cause I don't think we can carry it back down."

I cleared my throat. "Um . . . what is it?"

Olivia sat up, laughing. "You can't tell?"

I inspected the pile of metal a little more closely. "It looks like scrap car parts."

Olivia nodded enthusiastically. "It is! I got this old junker for parts to fix mine. And the rest of the shell was just lying around collecting dust. So I thought I might make something out of the scraps, you know?"

She had taken the two pink doors of the old Chevy and put them on the front of a cabinet cut in their exact shape.

"Here, let's try putting it over in that corner," she said,

pointing to where the bobblehead box was. I helped scoot it out of the way as Dad and Olivia moved the cabinet into place. "Oh, can't forget this," she said, swinging an electrical cord around and then plugging it in. The headlights that were mounted inside the cabinet buzzed to life. It was a work of art. It was weird and fun and functional and creative. It was the perfect finishing touch to our Team Gravy project.

Olivia whispered to my dad through clenched teeth, "Does she hate it? I can't tell if she hates it?"

I realized my chin was wobbling and my eyes were leaking. Before I could start ugly crying, I ran over and threw my arms around Olivia and then Dad. "I love it. It is absolutely perfect. Thank you so much!"

I spent the rest of the afternoon putting my presidential bobbleheads in order in their perfect new space, and I wondered how long they might have lived in a box if Olivia hadn't joined the project.

36

All's Fair in Love

"It was November 26, 1904, when Teddy Roosevelt visited the Louisiana Purchase Exposition in St. Louis," Dad said.

"Otherwise known as the World's Fair," I interjected. We walked through the throng of people crammed into Forest Park and tried to stay arm in arm. Olivia and I twirled lacy parasols and Dad smiled sideways as he rambled on. People pointed and stared and I nodded and smiled in return.

The festival buzzed around us. Both sides of the walkway were lined with white vendor tents. Smells of delicious foods wafted through the air. Wearing my Alice Roosevelt costume, walking in a chain with my dad, dressed as Teddy, and Olivia, who made an excellent Edith, every once in a while it all felt real. Like we'd stumbled back in time and we were experiencing the fair just like the Roosevelt family had. The morning had been spent with crowds surrounding us, asking for pictures. We were as popular as the real First Family when they visited the fair in 1904!

"You know, many of the things we see here today would have been modern wonders at the 1904 World's Fair." Olivia's voice was smooth as velvet. "Hamburgers, hot dogs, iced tea . . ." She paused for dramatic effect. "Ice cream cones!"

I could listen to her talk about history all day. She had a way of telling stories that made me want to fall right in.

Dad continued, "One of the more interesting things you could see in the sculptures palace—"

Olivia interrupted. "A butter sculpture of Teddy Roosevelt!" It was cute the way they finished each other's sentences.

We'd stopped in front of what was now the Saint Louis Art Museum. The fancy building had been built just to hold sculptures at St. Louis's first World's Fair. "Hey, is this the place?" I asked. Dad consulted the faded black-and-white photograph and then nodded. "I believe it is."

My heart thudded in my chest. This was the moment we'd been waiting for.

The sun beat down on the top of my flat bonnet, and the wind tickled the stray hairs curving out around my ears, but I stood as straight and proper as I could and tried not to move a muscle.

"Shift your parasol just a little to the left," Dad said, holding up the old photo we were trying to re-create.

I inched the shade to the left and blinked into the sun, smiling so hard my face felt like it might crack.

"Perfect," Dad said after clicking the picture. "Come see."

From the moment this picture had drifted out of the journal in the attic, I'd wanted to re-create it. Today we were doing it.

"You are just as pretty as she was," Dad said, grinning.

"It looks perfect," Olivia said, smiling at the back of the camera. She wore a frilly white dress with a high neckline, quite stylish for 1904. She had a flattish sort of bonnet tied to her head, too. When we'd asked her if she wanted to come with us while we reenacted Teddy and Alice's visit, she'd agreed at once and started on her Edith costume in the next breath. We looked like the first family, minus Alice's five younger brothers and sisters.

We laughed and talked and filled our bellies with the soft-serve Dad bought from a cart. I was sweating so much in my dress it felt like I'd jumped in the giant fountain we'd passed. In fact, I considered doing just that, except then my Alice costume might get ruined, and it was my prized possession. It had taken us weeks to get it exactly right. We'd done it all ourselves, with Olivia's help, of course, and it looked impeccable. It was the perfect dress for a fine young lady at the turn of the century, be it Alice Roosevelt or my four-times-great-grandma.

"Let's stroll over to the antiques appraisal booth," Dad said, smoothing his fake bushy mustache and adjusting his tie. Tiny round glasses perched on his nose, and his pocket watch chain glinted in the sunlight.

We were jostled among the crowd but managed to stay together until we found ourselves outside a white tent that said TRASH OR TREASURE? on its large blue sign.

A couple of people milled around the booth, squinting at the small signs accompanying the antiques. A very round man with a smile that turned his whole face pink sauntered over to us.

My dad straightened his spine. "Good day, sir. I wondered if you could appraise some historical documents for me?" The heavy wool suit made sweat bead on Dad's forehead, but he looked more excited than I'd seen him in a long time.

The big pink guy introduced himself as Tom and looked eager to get his hands on whatever the guy in the Teddy Roosevelt costume was about to produce.

Dad took a pile of letters out of his pocket. He unfolded the first one, but instead of leaning over it with Tom, he looked only at Olivia as he read it. "This is a letter from Ronald Reagan to Nancy Reagan. He says, *I more than love* you, *I'm not whole without you. You are life itself to me. When you are gone I'm waiting for you to return so I can start living again.*"

Olivia clutched at the high neck of her dress.

Tom squinted at the paper. "Sir, that letter isn't even handwritten. It's just printed off the internet."

Dad was almost as pink as Tom. "Okay, what about this one? This is a verifiable letter from Lyndon B. Johnson to Lady Bird Johnson. He writes, *This morning I'm ambitious, proud, energetic and very madly in love with you.*"

Dad and Olivia were in a serious eyeball lock and I bounced on my heels.

Tom broke the trance. "Um . . . Mr. Roosevelt, sir, that letter is also a fake, I'm sorry to tell you."

"One more," Dad said, never taking his eyes off Olivia. "This last one has got to be worth something. It is a letter from Harry Truman to Bess Truman. *I suppose that I am too crazy about you anyway. Every time I see you I get more so if it is possible. I know I haven't any right to but there are certain things that can't be helped and that is one of them. I wouldn't help it if I could you know.*"

I handed a stunned-looking Tom a camera and whispered, "Get ready to take a picture."

"Such romantic words," Olivia murmured.

"A man, even a fake president, has to be romantic when

he is about to put his heart on the line." Dad dropped to one knee, and my hand flew to my mouth to cover up the giggles I felt bubbling out.

This was it. The plan we'd been working on for weeks. I felt my heart flutter in my chest. Olivia's lips were wiggling, like she was trying hard to keep them in a straight line, and I imagined her knees were knocking together under her lacy skirt.

"Olivia Jane O'Connor, I have a question to ask you."

I clapped my hands together and held my breath. Dad had been practicing what he would say to Olivia in the mirror for weeks, but it sounded much better with his voice all wobbly like it was.

She looked at him, her eyes wide with surprise, and waited for what he had to say.

"I wondered if you would do us the great honor of joining our family. Would you be my wife?"

He opened a small black box and held it out to her as an offering.

For a few seconds, which felt like a million years, everyone just froze. Then Tom looked over the top of the camera and asked, "Well, what do you say, ma'am?"

Olivia could barely get the words out, because she was laughing and crying at the same time. "Yes! Yes! Yes!"

She pulled Dad off his knee and into her arms in one gentle tug. *Snap.* Tom grinned and clicked away on the camera.

I watched them with a silly smile on my face until both of them reached out and yanked me into the circle. We hugged and laughed and Olivia and Dad both wiped at their tears. She pulled away for a second and looked me in the eyes. "Is this what you want too, Grace?" I smiled and nodded because I couldn't push any words out past the huge lump in my throat. "I know what you have with your dad is exceptionally special, and I would never want to get in the middle of you two. . . ."

"You aren't breaking up Team Gravy," I choked out. "You're joining Team *Groovy*. Grace plus Olivia O'Connor plus Davy."

Olivia threw her head back and laughed. "I've never been happier to join a team," she said. There was nothing I wanted more than for her to stay with us forever. She slid the ring on her finger and it was a perfect fit.

ACKNOWLEDGMENTS

Many hands helped shape this story, and I would like to take a moment to thank them.

To my lovely, gutsy, smart, and tough agent, Kate Testerman, thank you for setting this dream in motion.

To Caroline Abbey, my wonderful editor at Random House, thank you for seeing the direction that this story could take and helping me steer it there. You make things shinier.

To Polo Orozco and Barbara Bakowski, who read and contributed to this book, and to everyone else at Team Random House, thank you from the bottom of my gravy boat.

To Michelle Cunningham, thank you for creating the perfect invitation for kiddos to grab my book.

To the Woodneath Writers Group, the Woodneath Library Center, the Pitch Wars family, and the Twitter writing community, thank you for your continued support.

To Cassandra Miller, Malayna Evans, Stacy Hackney,

Carrie Allen, Shelly Steig, Kristina Rinard, Nancy Banks, Karen Mahara, and Taylor Ford, thanks for all the stupendous thoughts and comments. You all make me better at this whole writing thing.

To all my friends and family, thanks for your amazing support of my debut. You guys have a way of completely inflating my ego and keeping me grounded at the same time. And a big thank-you to my mom, Sherry Brummett. Sorry that the mom in this book is dead. No offense.

To Carrie Chambers, who is by far my biggest cheerleader: You might even have bigger writing goals for me than I do, and I love that about you. Thank you for sharing my work with your students with so much enthusiasm that they can't help but be superfans!

To Jennie Booth, I feel like your name should be on this book's cover for the umpteen-million times you have read it! Thank you for always reading my roughest drafts and lying about how good they are. You are the bestest.

And to Caleb, Loralie, and Roman: Love you three with all my heart.

ABOUT THE AUTHOR

© Kate Testerman

Niki Lenz is an author living in Kansas City, Missouri. She is married to a handsome and brave police officer and has two adorable children. She studied elementary education at Southwest Baptist University and taught kindergarten for six years. She enjoys reading, travel, glamping, polka dots, red lipstick, and oldies music. She is also the author of *Bernice Buttman, Model Citizen.*

nikilenz.com